If there was ever a hell, he knew this was it.

The creatures of the guano pit were of astonishing proportions: eight-foot diamondbacks, two-foot centipedes, foot-long spiders, scorpions, and beetles. The slime teemed with moiling killers.

Stanley assumed they would head back, when to his horror and dismay Torn Slater unlimbered a hundred feet of climbing line and snaked a long swirling loop across the sinkhole.

"The line's guaranteed for a thousand pounds. We each have belt clips to hook us on. I'll cross first." Hanging from the line by his hands and feet, Slater started over the abyss.

Waiting at the precipice's edge, explorer Henry Morton Stanley had never been so terrified in his life. When his turn came, the vampires were shrilling nervously, puzzled at the disturbance below. Paralyzed with terror, it was all he could do to clip on the belt-lock and swing out over the void into the blinding cyclone of bat excrement.

Then, three quarters of the way across the abyss, it happened. It appeared to him first like a black bloody mortar dropping from the sky—except that this shell had a wing-span of over two feet...

Novels by
JACKSON CAIN

Hellbreak Country

Savage Blood

Hangman's Whip

Hell Hound

Devil's Sting

Published by
WARNER BOOKS

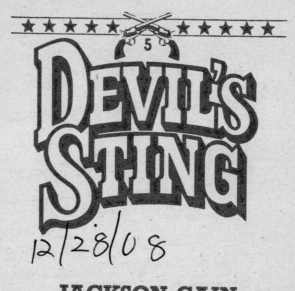

DEVIL'S STING

5

12/28/08

JACKSON CAIN

To Blaine,
who was born with
the gift of laughter
and a sense that the
world is mad.

Semper fi
Polar Bear

Jackson
Cain

WARNER BOOKS

A Warner Communications Company

This novel is a work of fiction. Names, characters, dialogue, places, and incidents are either the product of the author's imagination or, if real, are used fictitiously.

WARNER BOOKS EDITION

Warner Books, Inc.
666 Fifth Avenue
New York, N.Y. 10103

 A Warner Communications Company

Printed in the United States of America

First Printing: April, 1985

10 9 8 7 6 5 4 3 2 1

Special thanks to

Tom Corvell, Mike Garner, Jim Maddox,
Gene Meader, Wayland Mitchell,
Norm Woodard—and, last but not least,
Wild Bill Parnell

for helping me out with Jake Logan
and taking a chance on Jackson Cain

I am indebted to Robert Gleason and John Kelly for permission to quote from their songs, "Calamity," "Belle Starr, the Bandit Queen" and "Yuma Jail" on pp. 33, 75–7 and 263–4. Their work has provided the basic text for J. P. Paxton's "The Ballad of Outlaw Torn Slater" and has been a constant inspiration to me throughout the writing of these books.

BOOK I

No, I'll give you your revenge another time, when you are not so indifferent; you are thinking of something else now, and play too negligently. The coldness of a losing gamester lessens the pleasure of the winner. I'd no more play with a man that slighted his ill fortune than I'd make love to a woman who undervalued the loss of her reputation.

—William Congreve, *The Way of the World*

PART I

You know, Sutherland once told me that torture was "an expressive art"?
—Henry M. Stanley, explorer and journalist

1

Henry M. Stanley, the famed journalist and explorer, stood for a long moment by the altar at Saint Paul's Church of the Divine in New York City. He was dressed in a handsome black frock coat, with a matching vest and a bowler hat.

He felt relieved.

After all, the day before, his old nemesis James Sutherland was reported in the *New York Herald* as deceased, and soon he would gaze on him in his coffin.

Behind the altar a priest was presenting the Eucharist to a dozen communicants. He conducted his office with magisterial dignity. The mitre was high on his head. The long, flowing cope of crimson silk was draped gracefully around his shoulders, and his crooklike crozier hung loosely in his hand.

For a long moment Stanley considered taking Communion, but it was not to be. For one thing,

DEVIL'S STING

Henry Stanley was not of the Faith. For another, he had bloody business to attend to, the verification of an old enemy's death.

He swung his head around the vast stone vault of the cathedral, searching for Sutherland's coffin. He saw it. In the northwest corner in a circular alcove lay an open coffin. Behind it an altar blazed with candles. At the alcove's rear, a curved stained-glass window, depicting Christ's passion, faced the Hudson River. The bright noonday sun filtered through the colored glass, splashing a splendid rainbow of reds, blues, yellows and greens over the deceased. The niche looked serenely beatific.

Stanley turned from the altar and strode purposefully toward Sutherland's casket.

He hoped and prayed he would find him dead.

2

For a long moment Stanley stood before the funeral altar. He stared into the simple gray steel coffin. It was lined with pale blue velvet and its occupant was laid out in a black store-bought suit.

For a man of Sutherland's prodigious wealth, the affair was remarkably cheap.

But none of this concerned Stanley. All he wanted to know was whether the occupant was James Sutherland, and he most certainly was. There was no mistaking *that*. The glittering madman's eyes, the twisted sneer, half-grin, half-grimace; even the slick swathe of scar tissue streaking the right side of his pate, white and hairless as porcelain—the swatch of scalp which Torn Slater had lifted from him so long ago in those red-hot Sonoran canyonlands.

Stanley was jerked from his reverie by a discreet shoulder tap. He turned to face two bearded gentlemen—one old, the other late middle-aged. Both had hard eyes, heavily lined faces and were attired in black suits—generals William Tecumseh Sherman and Philip Henry Sheridan.

"You here to honor the grateful dead?" Sherman said in hushed tones.

"Never knew him to be grateful or honorable," Stanley said.

"Oh, I see. The vultures come home to roost." Sherman nodded. "I didn't even believe he was dead. Guess I figured he was too mean to die. Or that the whole thing was a hoax."

"You believe it now?" Sheridan asked, staring at the deceased.

"For sure. Nothing that ugly could be cooked up."

Stanley returned his gaze to the coffin. Again, he studied the crazed eyes, the crooked sneer, the half-scalped pate.

A grinning ghoul, he thought with a shudder.

"I hear you two did business with him," Stanley finally said.

"The military did. Guns, uniforms, transport, ammunition. You name it, he sold it. Outfitted half the Army of the Potomac back in the Rebellion. After that he sutlered and equipped most of the Indian campaigns. Had a lock on it. On everything."

"Must have been nice."

"Like shaking hands with the devil."

"Like backing into a buzz saw bare-ass naked," Sheridan said with a touch of frontier profanity.

"He was mean enough to kill Jesus."

Stanley turned to face the speaker behind him. The man was wearing a well-cut dark blue three-piece suit with a matching bowler. He had a square peasant's face, a broad black mustache and eyes pale and expressionless as blue ice. His mouth was hooked into a cramped smile.

John Pierpont Morgan.

"J. P.," Sherman said.

The three of them quietly shook hands with the richest man on earth.

"You also here to identify the remains?" Sheridan asked.

The mighty Morgan cringed. "Am I ever. I'd've rather seen him flogged, castrated, quartered and cremated. And a stake driven through his ashes. But this'll do."

"I take it you also had business dealings with him?" Sheridan asked.

"I did. Rockefeller did. Carnegie did. The bastard got into Wall Street six or seven years back, and we decided to teach him a lesson in humility. When the three of us gang up on an investor, it's hard for him to come out on top."

"You wiped him out?" Stanley asked.

"He cleaned *our* clocks. Stock frauds, bond manipulations, bribery, kickbacks, industrial sabotage, everything. He used every trick in the book against us, many of which we thought we'd invented ourselves."

"Like what?" Stanley asked.

"He conned five of our associates into hotel rooms with women. He nailed them with the old badger game and bled them white as old bones. Tortured them halfway to death with those hideous photographs. Naturally, he forced the poor buggers to sell us out. Later on, he almost drove John D. to suicide. Carnegie he nearly killed. Two we proved he did kill, but just before the indictment he had our Pinkertons assassinated and purloined the evidence."

"He was known to be a little greedy," Stanley said wryly.

Morgan shot him a hard look. "He didn't just kill the golden goose, he butt-fucked it first."

Sherman emitted a low, appreciative whistle. "Was that little encounter expensive?"

"John D., Carnegie and myself wrote off a hundred million apiece. We considered ourselves lucky. After all, we got out with our lives."

Slowly, almost hypnotically, all four men turned back toward Sutherland. There he lay. The perpetually grimaced sneer, the half-scalped alabaster pate. He was decked out in a poorly made suit and ensconced in a cheap coffin.

"God," Morgan groaned, "just looking at something that horrible could kill you."

Stanley patted Morgan's shoulder in consolation. "You know, he once told me that torture was 'an expressive art'?"

"He expressed that sentiment often," Morgan said.

"With astonishing clarity," Sheridan added.

Stanley reached into his hip pocket. He produced a hammered silver brandy flask with the initials H.M.S. lavishly engraved on it in Gothic script. He poured a large draught into the two-jigger cap and tossed it off. He helped himself to another. When he looked up, he caught the other men staring at him.

"It's for an old diamondback bite," he said.

"Control yourself, man," said Sherman, pointing to Stanley's shaking hands. "You're white as a winding sheet. You can't still be terrified of him. He's dead."

Stanley shook his head. "He threatened me once for something I had written about him. Understand, I'm no coward. I discovered the source of the Congo River, fought for the Congo Free State and tracked down Livingstone. But also know that the threat he made—which was most direct and obscene, followed by the look in those utterly unforgettable eyes—well, I published a retraction instantly over an article which was both true and harmless. So, yes, I was afraid of him. Perhaps I still am. And, yes, his death means a great deal to me."

But now Sheridan was distracted. "Did you get a look at her?" he said, staring at the bereaved fiancée in the black mourning dress standing a discreet distance from the funeral niche.

They all nodded. It was hard to ignore Judith McKillian. She stood alone, hips canted, thumbs hooked inside an 18-karat gold-chain belt. Her glossy mane of flame-red hair fell casually over her shoulders and down her back almost to her ass. Her mourning dress was of jet-black gossamer-sheer silk; and a soft, brief swatch of mourning lace fell elegantly over her head. She wore dark heels and stockings. A massive emerald, pinned to a pitch-black garter, adorned her throat. An array of gold rings, studded with rubies and sapphires, glittered on her fingers.

Stanley's eyes slowly ascended to her face. Flawless buttermilk skin. High flaring cheekbones. The most brilliant emerald eyes he'd ever seen. A wide generous mouth.

Slowly, she turned her head, and suddenly she was

staring at him, her flashing eyes filled with sin and wickedness.

Stanley's hands began to shake, and he averted his gaze.

When he finally had the nerve to look at her again, she was staring out into space.

A grin of triumph crooked her mouth.

3

While Stanley stood dumbstruck, the other three continued their talk. Morgan was saying confidentially, "I hear she inherited a substantial piece of his fortune."

"I hear she's a substantial piece herself," Sheridan said.

"She was allegedly fucking the milkman," Morgan said.

"She was probably fucking the milkman's horse," Sherman observed coarsely.

"I don't care," Sheridan said, looking at the McKillian woman. "I'd still like a crack at his girl. She makes me think of one of those gory-locked priestesses of old. Eyes blazing, snakes writhing in her hair, a blood-guttered axe flashing in her fist."

"How'd she tie up with Sutherland?" Stanley asked.

"The usual reasons. Money. Danger. Power. She

saw him as a sword against the world," Sherman said.

"A falcon on her glove," Stanley offered.

"Exactly," said Sherman. "Then one day they ran into a real bird of prey."

"What happened?" Morgan asked, interested.

"This new bird supposedly dumped them in a well, dropped a hive of bees on them and sealed off the top."

"It's surprising any of them survived," Morgan said.

"Sutherland never did. Not really. It broke his spirit. A man like him is nothing without all that crazed furious energy. He lasted about six months. They say he found God near the end."

"I somehow can't picture it," Sheridan said.

Sherman nodded his agreement.

"Who was this bird of prey?" Morgan asked. "The one who threw our priestess in the well? And killed her bloody falcon?"

"He was *muy hombre*, all right," much man. "He was one whom the Sioux call *Hunka Wambli*, or Spirit-Eagle. In fact, he was a big bloody bastard of an eagle. He was the one us white-eyes call Torn Slater."

"Is he as bad as they say?" Morgan asked.

"Story goes he did for two dozen Comancheros before putting those others in the well."

"Did any of you know him?" Morgan wondered.

"I didn't," Stanley said, "but Bill Hickok did. To hear him tell it, Slater was a walking apocalypse. 'A little worse than Armageddon' was the way he phrased it."

Sheridan was staring at the McKillian woman. "I'd

still like a shot at her."

"You're one hard rock, Sheridan," said Morgan, shaking his head. "Even so, I'd recommend you hold your spurs."

"What she needs," Sherman said, smiling, "is an older man. Someone with a firm hand. Someone who knows his way around the female of the species. Someone with more than six decades of proven expertise. Someone who would make her toe the mark, who would keep her in line. Someone like me."

"How would you keep her in line?" J. P. Morgan asked, looking the old man up and down derisively. "Spank her with your truss?"

"If I had to. She looks hotter than a hickory fire."

Stanley was staring once more at Sutherland's face. "I don't care what you say. Just look at him. That man once scared the buffalo chips out of me."

"He could have taught the Apaches to fight dirty," Sheridan agreed.

J. P. Morgan cleared his throat. "Any of you hear what's happening to his fortune?"

"A lot of it's invested in Mexico," Sherman said.

"What did he find down there?" Stanley asked.

"Mexicans."

"No, really."

"Really. He acquired a virtual army of them, built an empire. Slave-labor mines. Slave-labor haciendas. Slave-labor factories. In return, he helped Diaz finance railroads, oil fields and industrialization. Both men were making fortunes when he died."

"I hear their national bird is the fly," Sheridan said.

"They say America's the vulture," Stanley replied.

"That's our country you're insulting, boy," Sherman said, relieving Stanley of his flask and tapping it for a drink.

"Sorry, General. Didn't mean to spit on Old Glory."

Slowly, Sheridan took out his gold Elgin. It had a hinged lid, a ten-day movement, and the key dangled from the chain. Even as the general studied the watch face, Stanley could read the upside-down anachronistic *IIII*.

"I guess it's about that time," Sheridan said.

"Well, be good, Jimmy, wherever you are," Sherman said.

"I'm afraid we all know where that is," J. P. Morgan observed tersely.

"Yes, I just can't picture him in heaven strumming lutes and hip-harps," Stanley concurred.

"Come on, lads," Sherman said, lifting the flask, "words have to be said for the old boy. Nothing mawkish either, seeing as how we're all agreed on the place to where he's going."

Sheridan took the flask from Sherman, had a discreet snort, then raised the flagon in toast. He intoned solemnly:

> Oh Dis, our God of ancient stones,
> Our sacred song for thee atones.
> We drink thy blood in loving cups
> And break for thee men's bones.

As Sheridan attempted to invert the bottle once more, Morgan twisted it out of his fist.

"Jimmy would have liked that," J. P. Morgan said, lifting the liquor.

"Yes, but he's dead now," Sherman said.

"I like to think that he just got bucked out of the chute," Sheridan offered.

"No, he's gone home for good," Morgan said.

Sheridan nodded his agreement. "You take it slow, Jimmy."

"Yeah," Stanley said, "and shake it easy."

4

All in all, it wasn't a bad service. Stanley enjoyed the
litany, the doxology, the two hymns—"Holy, Holy,
Holy" and "Oh, God, the Rock of Ages"—and he was
more than a little impressed by the priest who was
the same dignified clergyman whom he'd watched
earlier. The one with the mitre high on his head, the
long flowing crimson cope draped elegantly over his
shoulders, the crooklike crozier now gripped tightly
in his fist.

However, in some respects, his sermon on Sutherland was a little much.

Oh, the beginning was plausible. The priest spoke
of how Sutherland had first visited his confessional
as a kind of bizarre practical joke. He wished to
confess to sins of mockery and blasphemy, and then
Sutherland had proceeded to inflict on the poor
man the worst blasphemies his twisted mind could
contrive.

Yes, that definitely sounded like Sutherland, but the next part had Stanley stumped. Sutherland seeing the Light? And praying for redemption?

"For James Sutherland saw before him his death and judgment," the priest eulogized. "In his vision he saw his own remains hammered into a box and lowered into the grave. He saw himself trembling before Christ's Judgment Seat. And he knew hell was near.

"For this was a man whose time was spent drinking and whoring, robbing and killing. This was a man who knew the wicked way of all Satan's sins: greed, carnality, pride, envy, sloth, intemperance, ire, deceit and murder-most-foul. His life was a mockery of God's plan, of His holy sacraments, of His divine testament and prayers.

"But now in his vision, it was Christ's day. Each of Sutherland's sins came shrieking forth before the Judgment Seat. The moon turned to blood. The stars went out. Christ was no longer meek and mild. He was the Divine Justicer, the Eternal Scourge. Christ's words thundered through Sutherland's soul: *Depart from me into hell's eternal fire! All art gone! Thou art gone! Abandon all hope, thou who scorned the Lord!*

"And Sutherland was driven into hell's blackness. He wallowed in the bottomless pit where balefire rages and where bodies writhe eternally; and where in pitchy flames, hell's lost souls wail forever their despair.

"All were dead. All were adjudged. All were cursed. And now Sutherland knew. *Repent*, His conscience cried. *Repent and be saved. In meek abnegation, in heartfelt genuflection.*

"Kneeling in that confessional, he looked up at the

crucifix. And his God stared down on him in bloody tears and sad-eyed wonder from the gaudy gibbet of His Cross.

"Throughout his life, Sutherland's soul had responded to nothing more than lurid tinglings of the flesh and the chiming echoes of a cash register's din. But that was changed. This child of wrath, this tiger of the night had consecrated himself to the Father Who created him, the Son Who had lifted him up and the Holy Spirit Who had made him whole. He yearned only for a life devoid of possessions and longings and the world's sinful snares. His heart trembled; his spirit soared; he was purged and purified by grace.

"In a still, small voice he told me he would bequeath it all.

"All those worldly things which had brought him only hatred, grief, despair and death...

"To God.

"Sutherland was alone now. He was joyful, free, close to the throbbing pulse of Eternal Grace. He was wonder-filled and glorious of soul. Sacred silence enveloped him. His spirit trembled, moaned, swooned. And he went to meet his God."

The cathedral was still as a tomb.

Stanley stared at the priest in dumbstruck disbelief. Did the words mean what he thought they meant?

He looked to his friends for confirmation.

It was so.

J. P. Morgan, the richest man on earth, had passed out cold from the shock.

5

The four friends were making their way down the church steps. They were stopped by Father Tibbs and a tall, aristocratic gentleman in a fashionably cut suit of raw black silk.

"Mr. Stanley? Henry Morton Stanley?"

The four men turned and shook the priest's out-stretched hand.

"I'd like you to meet my friend, Robert P. Hargrove, attorney-at-law."

The other three quickly introduced themselves.

"I noticed you gentlemen by the casket, then later in your pew. When four men such as yourselves give up so much of your valuable time, it can only mean you loved the deceased very much."

The four men stared at him incredulously.

"Mr. Sutherland had so much love in him. You four understood that, didn't you? The love he felt for others?"

"He loved people the way wolves love baby lambs," Sherman said.

Father Tibbs attempted to disagree, but Sheridan cut him off. "Father, let's be frank. What he said on his deathbed don't mean squat. I *knew* Sutherland. He was a carnivore, and he craved the taste of blood. That was all."

"Just the way you like your Indians?" Lawyer Hargrove conjectured.

"You got it, Counselor. Dead and in the ground," Sheridan answered truthfully.

Father Tibbs cleared his throat nervously. "Now, gentlemen, a small favor. Mr. Sutherland stated in his last will and testament that while most of his money was to go to charity and the Church, he wanted to leave a small bequest to a few particular friends whom he'd wronged. Lawyer Hargrove and I are to track them down for the reading of the will. Mr. Sutherland was adamant that they attend the reading, and we are sworn to carry out his last wish. I have a list of their names. I believe, Mr. Stanley, you know a number of them."

He showed the four men the list.

> Sitting Bull
> Buffalo Bill Cody
> Calamity Jane Cannary
> Geronimo
> Sitting Bull
> Porfirio Diaz
> Ned Buntline
> Cynthia Acheson
> Lord Percy Worthington
> Outlaw Torn Slater

Stanley nodded. "I can put you in touch with Cody and Calamity easy enough. Buntline's with Cody, and the two Indians are on reservations. You can track Percy and Cynthia through Belle Starr. She's got a place in the Nations at the fork of the Canadian and North Canadian Rivers. She can direct you to the lord and the countess. She or Clem could get through to Slater. If he wanted them to."

Lawyer Hargrove was making notes in a small vest pad. "That's good. Very good."

"Is there any way we could persuade you to help us track down these ten?" Lawyer Hargrove asked.

"No, I have to be going. I'm returning to Africa."

"We all have to be going," Sherman said.

Stanley turned to leave, when, glancing up the steps, he spotted the McKillian woman again, this time standing in the church doorway. She stood hip-cocked, thumbs in the gold-link belt, fiery hair wafting in the breeze, her eyes glinting with wickedness through her black lace mourning veil.

The eyes pinned him where he stood.

Phil Sheridan walked back up the steps and took him by the arm.

"Come on, bucko, you've had a little too much coffin varnish."

Stanley stood frozen on the spot, still staring at Judith McKillian.

At last, he turned and walked blindly down the steps.

The vision of the gory-locked pagan priestess—snakes writhing in her hair, teeth flashing, a blood guttered axe still blazing in her fist—was hotly etched in his mind.

PART II

Some say you leaned too hard on drink,
Some say you whored your ass.
From the righteous path you sure did shrink,
And that fast-track life don't last.
                    —J. P. Paxton, "Calamity"

6

A tall, willowy madam in a satin evening gown stood at the top of the stairs. Her auburn hair was shoulder length and the crimson dress was formfitted, of daring design, its neckline plunging recklessly. She stood hip-cocked, arms akimbo, her darting eyes counting the house.

The upstairs cribs were full, and all six of the downstairs draped-off boltholes were not only packed; the girls inside had the customers lined up three deep.

Calamity Jane was impressed. Her whore-ladies were doing a land-office business. The layouts at her four dozen gaming tables were overflowing with chips, greenbacks, pesos, Liberty heads, double eagles and towering stacks of 'dobe dollars. Blackjack, red dog, faro, keno, stud, draw, lowball, craps, roulette—all the tables swarmed with gents. Throughout the saloon cries of "Three little ladies!" "Ante's a buck!" "Read 'em and weep!" and "Seven on the red!" rang above the din. The ratcheting *whir!* of the big wheel, the clattering rattle of the bones, the soft *whisk-whisk, whisk-whisk* of the pasteboards flicking across the green baize of the seven- and eight-handed poker games and more cries of "Dealer pays!" "Twenty-one!" and "Big Casino!"

Calamity Jane's eyes swept over the crowd. It was time for her to mingle with the customers. Leisurely, she descended the stairs. Her bar-brothel was booming. She had every reason in the world to be pleased.

But, in truth, it meant nothing to her.

The woman was bored.

Calamity Jane Cannary missed her man.

Outlaw Torn Slater.

7

It was during her third pass around the main room that the somber-looking fellow in the dark suit approached her. The gent pointed to his table where a black-cowled priest was seated. He asked her if he could have a moment of her time to discuss business.

"Thanks for the encouragement, pard, but this lady don't turn 'em no more."

"That's not the business I was referring to."

"Nor do I have any plans of sellin' out."

"That's not it, either. Please."

Calamity shrugged, ordered up a bottle of sour mash from a passing daughter of joy and took a seat.

"Okay, Captain, it's your play."

Lawyer Hargrove discussed Sutherland's demise in some detail, then explained the terms of the will.

"You mean Torn and me both got to be there for the readin'? To collect?"

"Yes, ma'am."

"You say Sutherland found God?"

"Yes," Father Tibbs replied, "which is why he wanted the will read at *El Monasterio*. He felt it should be done in a Christian atmosphere. He wanted his heartfelt religiosity to come through."

Calamity shrugged. "Oh, I believe you. I suspect you'll have trouble convincin' some of them hard-case holdouts like Cody and Slater. But, hell, I've know'd a lotta men who seen the Light. They was all crazy toward the end."

Hargrove and Tibbs shot each other a glance.

"Any chance you could help us with Torn Slater?" Lawyer Hargrove asked.

"He's hard to get to, all right. I might be able to reach him on my own. After some of the shit he's been through, he just don't welcome strangers."

"Would you try to convince him to come?" Father Tibbs asked.

"*Padre,* you wanna know the truth, I'm damn sick of the whore-lady business. I'm also tired of patchin' up Slater every time he comes to me all shot to pieces. This money you talk of, hell, it could mean a whole new life for us. It could get me out of the whore-lady racket and get my man off the owlhoot. Which would be worth everything. Yeah, I'll try to talk him into it. 'Cause if'n he and I don't straighten our hands pretty soon, there won't be no cards left to play."

"It must be rough, loving a man like Mr. Slater," Father Tibbs said gently.

"He's got a lotta hard bark on him, *Padre.* And anymore, I just can't take the strain."

PART III

Mejico, she is not a very fair country.
                                    —Aquilar

8

A tall man stood on the black wrought iron balcony overlooking the main street of *El Carrizo*. His tan sweat-stained Plainsman's hat was slanted low over his eyes, shading them from the searing desert sun. His Levi's and collarless brown shirt were still dusty after the long ride from Chihuahua. The saddleless dun, tied to the hitch rack below, looked stove in.

His fine Appaloosa and his girl's roan were stabled up the street. They were enjoying rest and feed. The dun was either wind-broke or down with the contagion. The man would make up his mind which in a few more hours. If it was the former and not serious, the man would sell or trade him to a kindly-looking *peon*. If it was the latter, he would take him into the *llano*, give him a few kind words and put him down.

The man glanced up the dusty street. A scattering of two dozen adobe shacks baked in the fierce desert heat. The sun was at its zenith, and the few observable *peons* had already begun their afternoon siestas in the shade of their hovels and jacals. Otherwise nothing. No rising smoke, no breath of breeze, no horses or dogs or even the usual assortment of random chickens pecking at the road.

For the moment, *El Carrizo* was dead.

But only for the moment. *El Carrizo* was a *Mejicano* hurrah town, a south-of-the-border sink of iniquity waiting for sundown. *El Carrizo* seemed to exist solely as a stopping-off point, a limbo for wrongdoers and desperadoes, for men on the slippery slope to the infernal pit. In *El Carrizo* they paused long enough to *chinga* some *putas*, belt back the local mescal and enjoy a hand of cards.

Then, like diamondbacks at nightfall, they spat their foul poison and were gone.

The man up on the balcony squinted his flat black eyes as if expecting something or someone to disturb the town's dead-hot calm. As he did, the corners of his eyes split and cracked into a sun-darkened maze of deeply etched, alkali-streaked lines.

The hard inheritance of too many years in the arid *Mejicano llano*.

Slowly, the man turned on his heel and headed back into the hotel.

9

He had the best room. The thick adobe made it cool in the day and comfortable at night. It had a big feather tick, a wall coatrack and two bentwood chairs from the bar.

By *El Carrizo* standards, he was in the Presidential Suite of The Mark Hopkins.

But the man was not concerned with these furnishings. Instead, his gaze fell on the petite young thing flung across the bed, her lissome body twisted under the thin sheet in a tautly outlined, astonishingly sensual S-curve. Her eyes were closed, and her chest rose and fell so deeply and rhythmically that she looked as if she could sleep her way through Antietam.

She yawned and stretched. The slight movement gently tossed a dozen strands of her waist-length raven hair across her left cheek; several fell casually across the girl's wet, parted lips.

Remembering what she had done with those pouty

bee-stung lips less than an hour ago made the man's groin ache.

He turned his gaze to the petulant woman sitting in the bentwood chair to his right. Like him, she was dressed in trail garb: Levi's; a collarless tan shirt; a big cross-draw Colt; roweled boots; and a black Stetson, the band studded with conchos—all of it stained with sweat and dust. She had reddish brown hair pulled back into a tight ponytail, good bones, and, under the bulky clothes, the man knew she had a strong, shapely body. Long of leg. High of breast. Firm of bottom. And unlike his own flat, expressionless coal-black stare, her eyes promised merriment, good times and, if you were man enough, better ones to come.

But not now.

They had spent the better part of an hour fighting.

After one more look into those blazing brown orbs, he knew she was not done.

Slowly, Torn Slater began to massage his temples. The meeting—which *she* had demanded and arranged here in *El Carrizo*—had begun badly.

Calamity had walked in on him just as he was putting the blocks to that luscious young thing, groaning and writhing on the tick.

Yet even so, Slater's motives had been laudable. He had traveled to *Mejico* to liberate this young *puta* from a stone-cold, dog-mean pimp. That done, he was to transport her across the North American border. Up there—once she was safely out of the pimp's reach—an old friend would see that she was properly looked after.

Unfortunately, nothing is ever as simple as it seems. The dog-mean pimp also turned out to be a snake-mean *bandido*, and his pursuit was relentless.

It was now clear that Rozanna would never be safe from Aquilar and his four men.

Until Torn Slater killed them.

In *El Carrizo* he was determined to make his stand.

10

Slowly, Calamity Jane Cannary stood up. "I got the word on that boy what's on your back-trail. He ain't nothin' but hair, rattles and diamondback venom. 'Fore your girl passed out, she claimed he once ate a raw vulture and washed it down with panther piss."

"You don't like my plan none?"

"You call that a plan? Takin' on five outlaws with one belt gun?"

"It do skate like thin ice, don't it?" Slater said solemnly.

"Thinner'n cow piss on a flat fuckin' rock."

"Ain't nothin' I can say to make it any better."

"You could reconsider Sutherland's offer."

"Clem—"

"Now don't 'Clem' me. Sutherland's been in the ground five months, but before he went, he found his God. And he changed his will. And we're in it."

"Clem—"

"Now, damn you, it's bound to be worth a mint. All we gotta do to collect it is be at the readin'. It's down in that old Sonora monastery in the Sierras. You even been granted immunity. That Philadelphia lawyer promised."

"It ain't me. I never liked Sutherland. I even scalped him once. And hung him by the hocks over a slow-burnin' fire."

"Yeah? Then answer me this: Sutherland, he died rich and famous. His name was blazoned in newspaper headlines all over the West. And you? How'll you go? You'll die broke and alone, boot-buried in some wind-scoured boneyard, lucky to have a scrap-wood casket or get wrapped up in an old horsehide. Sutherland owned *countries*, and the only real estate you'll ever have is that six-foot hole they plant you in. No kids to sob, no wife to mourn your passin'. You'll die unknown in a pauper's grave. There won't be nobody there to care or to pull the grass up over your head." Calamity thumped her chest hard. "The same here. The same for me."

"That may be, but I ain't got no truck with Sutherland."

"You tellin' me you wouldn't take his cash?" Calamity asked, unbelieving.

"Sure I would. With his nuts in my fist and my red-hot smokin' Colt in his mouth. I'd *take* it from him. But I wouldn't go suckin' 'round after it."

"Bill Cody'll be there. Sitting Bull. Belle Starr. Geronimo. Buntline. Sutherland thought he wronged. It's okay for us to get rich, but not you. You too good for the money or something?"

"It ain't me. It ain't what I am. And it sure as shit ain't what I do."

11

Slater was packing his gear when Rozanna woke. She brushed the long raven hair out of her mouth and yawned. Calamity looked her up and down disdainfully.

"She any good?" Clem asked Slater.

"Like gettin' head from a hydrophobic bat."

"I also fucked his brains out," Rozanna added.

"Obviously," Calamity rasped.

"You two weren't fighting?" Rozanna asked. "I thought I heard you call him *el stupido*."

Clem looked at Slater appraisingly. "Him stupid? Hell, he has to tie a string to his dick just to find it. Has to tie it to the door handle to find his way out."

Rozanna stared at them quizzically, unsure about *gringo* humor. She looked back at Calamity. "Is he really so *stupido*?"

"Honey, you tell me. What's the story on them boyfriends of yours? Heard they got hands strong enough to straighten cold horseshoes. And rough enough to hammer fence posts into hard ground. Hear them five's mean enough to kill rocks. Well, this ole boy is takin' on all of them with one pissy belt gun."

Rozanna fixed Slater with a tight stare. "*Amigo*, that is not very smart. Do you use that gun well?"

"Naw," Calamity answered, "he don't use it at all. He just shouts magic chants at 'em and makes himself invisible."

Slater slowly got up from the other bentwood chair. He threw his saddlebags over his shoulder and headed toward the door.

"*Señor*," Rozanna asked, "is that all you have? That one gun?"

"'Fraid so."

"You will need more than that. Much more."

Slater looked at Calamity and smiled. A long slow smile. A smile to melt the hardest whore's heart.

Or turn an honest woman bad.

"I'd bring my Gatling but it stretches the holster."

He pushed open the door and headed for the stairs.

12

Time.

The wait seemed to take forever, but Slater was used to that.

Time.

Time was when you were captured by Apaches at the age of twelve and by the age of fifteen were leading raiding parties.

Time was leading the last charge at Shiloh, while ten thousand screaming Yankees shot your comrades to pieces. Time was turning away the overhanded thrust of a Yankee bayonet, blunting the attack with an elbow, and after putting a knee to the Yankee's crotch, breaking his wrist. Time was forcing him facedown into the Shiloh mud, shoving a knee into his back and, grabbing him by the throat and chin, wrenching hard on his head till—audible above the din of cannons and musket—you heard the dull *crack* of the breaking neck. Time was crawling back through the mud and muck and bursting shells to your own rebel trench, leaving the dead Yankee lying in a pool of your own blood.

Time was the years with Quantrill and Bloody Bill, looting and burning and above all murdering your way through Bloody Kansas and Bloodier Missouri. Time was riding with Frank and Jess and Coleman Younger after the War, sticking to banks and trains to vent your rage.

Time was the long years spent on the owlhoot trail and the longer ones in Yuma and Sonora prisons. In shackles and leg irons. On the long road doing hard time. Time was spent chained to the flogging post or locked in the hotbox or buried at the bottom of Diaz's slave-labor mines in the hideous Sulphur Shaft.

Time was having friends like Frank and Jess and Coleman Younger and Bill Hickok and Marquez and the old Doc. Time was looking down your back-trail and knowing that they were in jail or in the grave and there was nothing you could do to alter these facts.

Time was sitting at an empty cantina table, and on it, a big tricked-out Spanish saddle full of inlaid silver and turquoise and ebony leather. Time was carefully rubbing neat's-foot oil into the cantle and the leathers, making it look shiny and smooth, expensive and new for the five guests who would soon be walking through the front door.

With their guns.

Time was waiting.

Waiting without dread or hope or even fear. And where it would end, God only knew.

13

Up in the room, Clem sat with the Winchester straddling her knees.

"What do you think of *Señor* Slater?" Calamity asked Rozanna.

"When I think of him, I hurt *muy malo*."

"In your heart?"

"In my crotch."

"I don't know as I like that," Calamity said ruefully.

"So? *Señor* Slater, he no care you make love to your men."

Calamity shrugged. "He says men like him and Bill Hickok, they don't care."

"You say this Hickok, he screw you too? And *Señor* Slater no get jealous?"

"Only over *pesos*."

"That is good. When I go back to my profession, I would not want him angry at my *hombres*."

"Mean you ain't got no plans for reformin'?"

"After *Señor* Slater? *Madre Mia!* I could be the *Grande Puta* of *El Presidente*, Diaz. *Ey!* The things that man has shown me! They would be worth a fortune in *Mejico* City."

"Yeah," Calamity agreed, "when I walked in here, I half-expected firestorms, rock slides and eruptin' volcanoes."

"He is *muy hombre!*" Rozanna exclaimed.

"What the hell did your sister think you was? Something he could change from brothel-whore to fairy-tale princess with a kiss?"

"Bless her sacred soul, she was not practical."

"Does Slater know all this?"

"Not yet. I did not wish to hurt his feelings."

"Then maybe it's time to pull his coat."

She stood and started toward the door.

Then came to an abrupt stop.

Standing in her way was the biggest, meanest *bandido* she'd ever seen, nothing but teeth, beard and crisscrossed bandoliers.

"Hi, *bebe*," Aquilar said to Rozanna, "long time no see."

The gun leveled at Calamity's gut was Slater's Navy Colt.

14

Clem and Rozanna walked down the staircase into the cantina. Behind them, Aquilar came, prodding their backs and kidneys with Slater's gun.

As she descended, Clem surveyed the cantina with one swift glance. She did not see much. A dozen tables and chairs, and a raw plank bar serving mescal, *cerveza* and tequila.

Except for Slater sitting at his table and the four *bandidos* standing before him, the cantina was empty.

Halfway down the steps Aquilar shouted to his friends, "See, *amigos*, the famous Outlaw Torn Slater. He no look so tough now. Like a diamondback when you pull the fangs. He maybe rattle a little and whip his tail, but he got nothin' to bite with." Aquilar drunkenly waved Slater's Colt over his head.

One of the four in front of Slater was a *gringo*. His name was Jonas. He stepped foward.

"You got any prayers or last words? If you do, spit

them out. Once these boys get started, you ain't gonna feel like no acts of contrition."

Slater took this calmly.

Jonas grinned. "No sir. They're gonna take you down hard. Slow and hard."

Slater, still seated, continued to soap the fine Spanish saddle. It had a dinner-plate pommel, a high ornate cantle and was made of hand-tooled ebony leather heavily inlaid with silver and turquoise. The leather looked rich and expensive.

To Clem's irritation, Slater worked on it intently, oblivious to the men's threats.

Aquilar prodded the two women to the side of Slater's table while he joined his friends in front. When he reached them, he looked down at Slater. He smiled broadly.

"Amigo," he said to Slater, "I am afraid you and I, we got a minunderstanding. Is that not so?"

"You mean I'm in some sort of trouble?"

"Well, *amigo*," Aquilar answered, "you gonna die. Is that trouble?"

"Not till it happens."

"Hey," Aquilar asked, "can't you think of some better joke than your own death? I don't think your death she gonna be so funny." He pronounced it "fonny."

Slater looked up slowly.

"I got some good jokes 'bout Mexicans."

Aquilar's grin vanished. He stepped forward and grabbed the saddle's pommel, giving it a good shake. "What you doin', *amigo*? Sittin' here like some big pussy waitin' to get fucked, when you know you gonna die."

Slater glowered at the saddle, his forehead furrowed

in deep thought. "I haven't figured it out yet. I keep asking myself, 'What would Kit Carson do in a situation like this?'"

Again Aquilar laughed, this time spraying the fancy saddle with tobacco-stained spittle.

"If I'd wanted someone to drool on the saddle," Slater said, "I'd've brought a dog."

Aquilar stopped laughing. He straightened and gave Slater a hard look. Jonas eased up alongside him.

"Sure you ain't got no bond with the girl? You ain't married or nothin'. I'd purely hate to make her a widow so young and all."

"No ties stronger'n the come I left in her. And, hell, that's probably dribbling down her legs right now."

Aquilar's face reddened with rage. "You laugh, *gringo*, but that was my *mujer*," my woman, "you fuck and steal. So now I'm gonna have to take you down the hard way. You like that? *Ey?*"

"I like your red face, *cholo*."

"Yeah?"

"I'd like to light a whorehouse window with it."

Again, the *bandidos*, except for Aquilar, burst into laughter.

Aquilar bent over the table toward Slater.

"Tell me one thing. What you doin' here with that goddamn saddle?"

Slater shrugged. "I thought I'd give it to your girl. As a present."

"But she ain't my girl, but my *puta*," my whore. "So you gonna give it to me."

"Don't seem fair, seein' how she's the one that earned it."

"*Mejico*, she is not a very fair country."

Jonas leaned over the saddle. "Well, partner, I suggested alternatives. Maybe passin' the hat, sendin' you to charm school. Only, they got other plans." He slapped the gun butt on his hip. The piece was a no-shit Walker Colt, a pistol with the range and stopping power of a Henry rifle. It was the most powerful handgun made. A saddle gun, really, not meant to be slung on a hip but holstered on a horse.

"My friend," Aquilar said, "when I was a kid, I trapped a fly. I'd try to figure it out. When I couldn't figure it out, I'd tear its wings off, then its legs. That way, if I couldn't figure it out, I still feel *mucho bueno*," much better. "'Cause maybe I don't unnerstan' nothin', but that fly, he don't get around so good. You *sabe*? Same today. I can't figure somethin' out, I take it apart like that fuckin' fly. I can't figure you out, then I take you apart. Now. *Muy malo*. Very painful, very slow."

Jonas laughed uproariously.

Listening to his laughter, Slater felt something thump in his stomach. He placed his left hand on the back of the cantle and looked up at Jonas. "You know, where I grew up I was told there weren't nothin' lower'n sidewinder shit. Think I found somethin' lower'n that even."

"Lower'n diamondback droppins?" asked Jonas.

"Sure. You—you greaser-suckin' sonofabitch."

Shouldering Jonas aside, Aquilar shoved a finger in Slater's face.

"You push, *gringo*."

Slater gave Aquilar an elaborate shrug. "Yeah? Well, is it true your mama won first prize in an Abe Lincoln look-alike contest?"

Aquilar's hand flashed for his Colt. At the same moment, the other four *bandidos*, fanned out before the table, went for their sidearms.

But Slater had already made his move.

Slater's left hand, which had been soaping the cantle, grabbed it hard. The right stayed under the saddle fork, which it had been bracing.

At the precise moment that Aquilar's Colt cleared its holster, the front of the saddle—which was now levitating above the table—exploded in a blazing ball of red-orange fire. The edges of the saddle billowed with whitish black-powder smoke, and the saddle, despite its mass and bulk, kicked high above Slater's head.

The first barrel of the 8-gauge, cut-down Greener spat out two dozen lead balls, a quarter-inch in diameter apiece. Since the barrel beneath the saddle had been sawed off at the breech, they spread instantly. By the time they reached the *bandidos* standing eight feet from the table, their pattern was ten feet across.

When Slater lowered the saddle's charred, smoking remains, four of the *bandidos* were chopped to pieces. Only Jonas, off to the right, was still standing. He dropped his Walker Colt to the floor, threw up his arms and shouted: "Jesus, God! No! I'm a white man. Like yourself."

The expensive saddle, lavishly inlaid with silver and turquoise, burst into a smoke-shrouded sheet of flame.

A blast of buckshot blew Jonas into bloody eternity.

15

Outside the hotel, the three of them waited while the stable boy brought their saddled horses. Silently they vaulted their mounts. Slater dallied the packhorses' *mecate* once around his saddle horn, then looked at Clem.

"You comin' with us?"

"I'm goin' where the money is."

"That ain't my game. I don't feel like 'splainin' it twice."

Rozanna gazed at him fondly, nodding her head. "He is *muy hombre*," very manly. "Is that not so?"

"He ain't much. He knows how to kill men and rob trains. Otherwise he's got the brains of a sandbox."

"Clem."

"Don't Clem me. I ain't spendin' the rest of my life humpin' my ass like a government mule. I just ain't."

"Hell, I just give you half that money we found on them bandits."

"Jesus, you act like you earned it or somethin'."

"Didn't I?"

Calamity took out one of the hundred-dollar gold certificates she now had in her saddlebag.

"You even know whose picture's on a hundred-dollar gold certificate?"

Slater shrugged. "Roy Bean?"

"Guess again."

"Bat Masterson?"

Calamity looked away.

"Booker T. Washington?"

Calamity raked him with a cold stare.

"You mad 'cause of what happened in there?"

"Naw, you done it straight-up and head-to-head. I give you that. I just thought it'd be different. I thought you'd come along."

"I won't. I can't go suckin' after Sutherland. Alive or dead."

Slater glanced down. An ancient, grizzled derelict with a dusty, disheveled mustache, blood-streaked eyes and the filthiest sombrero Slater had ever seen was tugging at his stirrup leathers.

"Hey, *amigo*," the old derelict said, "you got some fine-looking *chiquitas*. I sure wish I had women like that."

Slater gave the foul-looking, foul-smelling drunk a searching stare. Then he glanced over at Calamity. "A man with your kind of looks? Hell, *amigo*, you shouldn't have no problem at all."

The old-timer shot him a wide, obscene grin full of broken yellow teeth.

"Damn you, Slater," Calamity said, eyeing Rozanna one last time. "Still beats the hell out of me why you'd settle for showers when you could have sheet lightnin', rollin' thunder and force-eight gales."

"It's my heart. I just can't take the strain no more."

"Then keep hell hot for me, you sissy sonofabitch."

Calamity wheeled her mount around and, waving her sombrero, loped on up the street toward Sonora and the old Sierra monastery.

PART IV

Amigos, I wouldn't cross that borderline into *Mejico* if there was a tidal wave of *pesos* in Tampico and a hurricane of hookers in *Veracruz.* Last time I dropped down there, Diaz squashed my tacos real good. So *Mejico* ain't seein' my worthless hide again. Not till Honest Abe rises from the dead and tells them rebs it was all a joke. Not till Jerusalem Slim comes back for an encore, gets busted for workin' miracles, without a license and dies in the saddle from too much good lovin'. I just ain't goin' back. Nohow.

—William F. "Buffalo Bill" Cody

16

Bill Cody leaned against the bar, hooking a boot heel on the brass foot rail. His "World-Famous Wild West Extravaganza" had deserted him just two weeks before—Ned Buntline absconding with the till—and now his situation was desperate.

Among other things, he had a dreadful case of the alcoholic shakes; and his empty belly felt wrapped around his backbone. His fringed elkhide jacket—bloodied along the bottom, charred from cook- and campfires along the sleeves—was soiled and frayed. His boots were rundown at the heels—one floppy-soled, the other minus a spur. His black felt sombrero with the three-foot brim and lavish gold embroidery was fast losing its shape. The ebony grip of his big Walker Colt was chipped, and he was missing three bullets. His goatee, mustache and long sandy hair were disheveled and ill-cut.

He lifted a shot of cheap pilgrim whiskey, and over

the rim of the glass he studied the Four Diamonds Saloon. The place was filling up fast with miners and cowhands, dudes and gents, town girls and daughters of joy, drifters and reputable businessmen. Most of the crowd—dressed in everything from trail garb to miner's denims, from claw-hammer coats to corsets and camisoles—mobbed the bar. The rest sat at the tables and chairs in front of the proscenium to see Cody's play.

The glass still hovering near his mouth, he turned to look over his shoulder at the big elevated stage. It was broad enough to hold a chorus of leg-kicking saloon girls and a twelve-piece orchestra.

Tonight it would hold him and the piano man.

The pilgrim whiskey hit the well of his belly like a howitzer, and he groaned silently. It was no wonder. Often such rotgut left men blind, crippled or even dead. As long as he'd been drinking it—in times like these when he couldn't afford the real stuff—he'd never gotten used to it.

Its only redeeming virtue was that it always left him drunk.

As Cody poured himself another shot, he painfully recalled how he had once stumbled onto a Chiricauhua camp. A bunch of Comancheros had sold them a keg of raw wood alcohol. It killed or blinded the men, and the Chiricauhua women—who were universally regarded as too violent and rebellious for the slave trade—were so totally subdued that they allowed themselves to be sold peacefully into Comanche slavery.

Cody tossed off the shot, winced, then reached for the rotgut.

When he saw it.

Right where his bottle of pilgrim whiskey had been.

A quart of twelve-year double-bonded triple-distilled Jack Daniel's whiskey.

17

Lawyer Hargrove stood up the bar from Cody with one fist in his pocket and the other around the neck of the Jack Daniel's bottle. Hargrove wore a tastefully cut brown suit with a matching bowler. His high cheekbones, granite-gray eyes, aquiline nose and haughty mien gave him an aristocratic look.

Beside him stood Father Tibbs. He was dressed in a black cambric cowl and a belt of hemp. He looked poised and self-contained.

"We've had the devil's own time finding you," Lawyer Hargrove said, pushing the bottle toward Cody.

Cody looked the two Easterners up and down and decided he did not like them. He stared at the Jack Daniel's bottle and debated turning the drink down.

The drink won.

"What the hell you want me for?" he asked, pouring himself a healthy slug.

"Your old friend and business backer, James Sutherland, has died. I presume you are aware?"

"Yeah, it was in all the papers. It was no great loss to the planet earth." Cody tossed back the shot.

"Well, his feelings toward you were a little more generous, I'm pleased to say."

"Yeah?" Cody was now reexamining the bottle with a shrewdly cocked eye, wondering whether it still worked.

He tried it again.

To his relief, it did.

"Yes, indeed. Toward the end, Mr. Sutherland led a spiritual life," Father Tibbs said gently. "He developed a close personal relationship with his Lord and Savior, Jesus Christ. He was redeemed. He came to believe most strongly in the power of love."

"When I knew Sutherland, all he believed in was rape, murder, torture and dismemberment. And makin' money. He believed real good in the long green."

"The *old* Sutherland," Lawyer Hargrove said, "had that unseemly love affair with money."

"He loved the *pesos*, all right. He played with them like they was his dick," agreed Cody.

"But in the end, he found God. He came to love his fellow man," Father Tibbs said.

"The Sutherland I knew, all he loved was inflictin' pain."

"Earlier in his life he had mistakenly adopted an eye-for-an-eye philosophy," Tibbs acknowledged sadly.

"A *head* for an eye was more like it. Sutherland didn't just make men sorry they'd messed with him. He made them sorry they'd been born on the same planet in the same century in the same universe. He made them curse their mamas for giving them birth."

"Sir, that all changed in the end," Lawyer Hargrove said. "He felt especially sorry for the countless times he wronged you. On his deathbed he sought to right those wrongs."

Cody's eyes were frankly incredulous.

"Mr. Cody," Lawyer Hargrove said, "as you know, the late Mr. Sutherland was a rich man. He chose to write you into his will. You're about to come into a very substantial inheritance."

"Yeah, and if you believe that, I have a terrific deal for you on reclaimed swampland in British Honduras."

"Please, Mr. Cody—"

"Don't shuck an old friend, *Padre*. Lookin' for Sutherland to cough up any of that scratch—alive or dead—is like lookin' for cherries in an Abilene whorehouse. That's just the way the shit shines. All he understood was *pesos* and pain. His *pesos*, and other people's pain."

"Toward the end he found his God," Lawyer Hargrove said.

"Yeah? Sitting Bull claimed Sutherland wasn't even human. Bull said he was snatched in his cradle by carnivorous butcher-birds. Claimed he was raised in a vulture roost on diamondback droppings and regurgitated carrion."

Father Tibbs shook his head disapprovingly as Cody tapped the bottle for his fourth straight shot.

"Mr. Cody, do you have a drinking problem?"

"I sure do, *Padre*. I'm hollow to my heels."

"Perhaps you should get some help."

"No thank-ee. I do right fine by myself."

Lawyer Hargrove took a deep breath and made his

offer. "Cody, in approximately six weeks there will be a reading of Mr. Sutherland's will down in the old Dominican monastery on *Sierra de Noche*. Mountain of the Night. Mr. Sutherland was most insistent that we have you and several of your friends there. He was adamant about your attendance. As a matter of fact, part of our own remuneration requires that we produce you."

"You say this old *monasterio* is down in *Mejico*?"

"In the Sonoran Sierras."

Cody's grimace was painful to the eye. "Friends, I wouldn't cross that borderline into *Mejico* if there was a tidal wave of *pesos* in Tampico and a hurricane of hookers in *Veracruz*."

"Mr. Cody, there is nothing to fear. Sutherland, among other things, is dead."

"Yeah? Well, the last time I was down there, that Diaz done fine all by himself. He squashed my tacos real good. *Mejico* ain't seein' my face again. Not till Honest Abe rises from the dead and tells them rebs it was all a joke. Not till Jerusalem Slim comes back for an encore, gets busted for workin' miracles without a license and dies in the saddle from too much good lovin'."

"Mr. Cody, please reconsider."

"Counselor, I wouldn't go into anything this crazy if I was free as a bird."

"Mr. Cody, all your friends will be there."

Cody showed the two men the backs of his hands. The first, second and third fingers on his left hand were missing nails. The rest were horribly scarred.

"Sutherland and Diaz had five of them nails pulled out. They would have yanked them all if Torn Slater hadn't stopped them."

The two men gave each other close looks.

"Perhaps you could help us with the whereabouts of this Mr. Slater. You do know him, I take it?"

" 'Bout the snakiest man I ever met."

"In which case, where might we find him?"

"Oh, I get it," Cody said with a cynical smile. "You're gonna sweet-talk me."

Lawyer Hargrove took out a massive black calfskin wallet and allowed Cody a discreet look. He riffled the bills. There were at least fifty one-hundred-dollar gold certificates in it.

"You're holding the paint cards," Cody admitted grudgingly.

Father Tibbs went on. "This land, like our souls is doomed and benighted. Brother Sutherland wished to see it redeemed by a joyous and loving God. We would really like to meet this Mr. Slater."

"What for? You need someone to charm a diamond-back? To cold-cock a cougar?"

"I believe all Mr. Slater really needs is honest, unselfish love," said Father Tibbs.

"Get him a dog."

"I meant spiritual love."

"That got something to do with homosexuality?"

"Mr. Cody, please don't blaspheme God's grace."

"Sorry, Sky Pilot, didn't mean to piss on your meal ticket. Anyway, Slater had a dog once."

"Yes?" Father Tibbs said politely.

"Damn thing was bigger'n Beelzebub and mean enough to rassle buzz saws. When Slater found it, some Comancheros was pittin' it against grizzlies, pumas and wild boars. Damn thing won, too."

"Must have gotten on fine with Slater," Lawyer Hargrove said.

"Crazy thing was, it did."

Cody helped himself to another drink.

Tibbs' face was a contorted mask of pain.

"Ah, that tastes like life itself."

By now the crowd was cheering. The piano accompanist was warming up.

Cody poured himself another belt.

"Mr. Cody, you must show restraint. You have a show to put on."

Cody tossed off the shot and poured another.

"Mr. Cody, you must show discipline. Iron discipline."

This time Cody helped himself right out of the neck of the bottle and belched.

The bottle in his fist, Cody started for the stage.

"Mr. Cody, I do think you have a drinking problem," Father Tibbs said nervously.

Heading for the stage, Cody yelled back over his shoulder, "I sure do, Sky Pilot. I'm thirsty as a hound dog in hell."

18

Cody waited in the wings for his host—Jamey Dunn, the Four Diamonds proprietor—to finish the introduction. Dunn looked quite elegant in his slate-gray claw-hammer coat, crimson cravat and black bowler.

Cody hoped Dunn's elegance would compensate for the absence of his troupe.

Which had skipped, weeks before.

Leaving him to face this pre-sold mob alone.

"So, ladies and gentlemen," Dunn proclaimed in ringing tones, "I want you all to give a grand welcome to that noble warrior of the high plains, that celebrated scout, soldier and Indian fighter, that exalted exemplar of man and boy worldwide—Buffalo Bill Cody!"

Cody slowly, haltingly, stumbled across the stage, the bottle of Jack Daniel's still in his fist.

The accompanist in the white boiled shirt, the red elbow garters and matching red bowler began banging out the refrain to Cody's first song, "Belle Starr, the Bandit Queen." Hands energetically pounding the ivories, a cigar clenched firmly in his teeth, the piano man finished the chorus and commenced the first stanza. Cody cleared his throat, and in a voice that was half-whiskey, half-monotone, he began to sing of the life of his friend Belle Starr.

> Eyes that burn like blazin' fire,
> Lips that taste like honey-dew.
> Mouth's a hot live lunging wire,
> Wayward, cunning and cruel.
> She'll twist you in the heat of desire
> Till you're beaten, broken, through.
>
> This wanton woman ain't no joke.
> She ain't no wild wet dream.
> This lady's born to break your heart
> And stomp it till it screams.
> The outlaw lady's very bad.
> The outlaw lady's mean.
> The outlaw lady's name's Belle Starr.
> Belle Starr's the bandit queen.
>
> She rode with Frank and Jesse James
> And Coleman Younger too.
> Cole's furious lust that girl inflamed
> While his baby in her grew.
> A violent life of riotous fame
> Just this side of the tomb.

At the phrase "Belle Starr's the Bandit Queen," Cody whipped out his six-gun and fired off three blanks at the spectators. Expecting an avalanche of enthusiastic cheers, he paused one or two pregnant seconds.

But the audience's response was neither enthusiastic nor cheerful. The audience was pissed.

"Where's the actors?" a drover in a big Stetson yelled. "And all them bare-naked women?"

A rather large miner in a red plaid cap and matching coat shouted, "You still got the bottle, Buffalo Breath! It's still in your fuckin' fist!"

And an indignant doxy screamed, "You're drunk, Buffalo Dick! Get off the stage!"

Nothing would have pleased Cody more, but the proprietor was holding Cody responsible for the $1100 worth of receipts out there.

Money for which Cody was liable.

Money which Cody could not return.

Cody glanced offstage. Dunn was pumping his arms in a circular motion, indicating that he should keep going. Dunn was also backed up by two rough-looking black-clad gents who glared menacingly at Cody with hard eyes, hip-braced scatterguns and shiny badges pinned to their chests.

The show must go on, Cody thought grimly.

Seventeen men took her for a wife.
Sixteen died by the gun.
That wild Cole Younger drew triple-life
His jailin' weren't no fun.
To be her man meant murder and strife
And a life spent on the run.

This wicked witch is slick as glass,
The heart of a filthy fiend.
A sweet soft mouth full of lyin' words
And the soul of a killin' machine.
The outlaw lady's very bad.

The outlaw lady's mean.
The outlaw lady's name's Belle Starr.
Belle Starr's the bandit queen.

Now the audience turned ugly.

"Get him off!" a drover hollered from the back of the room.

"Hey, Dunn, where's all the actresses and actors? The billboard says this is supposed to be a play, not Buffalo Chips singin' a bunch of drippy songs."

"Cody's drunk!" the outraged doxy screamed again.

Nervously, without thinking, Cody took a hard pull on his Jack Daniel's bottle. Now the boos and catcalls were thunderous, punctuated only by the floor-stamping and table-pounding. Still, Cody determined to put a good face on it. He pumped himself up and sang:

This little tramp's got sweet soft skin
And lips like your wildest dream.
But bloody death in either hand
And the coal-black heart of a fiend.
The outlaw lady's very bad.
The outlaw lady's mean.
The outlaw lady's name's Belle Starr.
Belle Starr's the bandit queen.

So sing of all them outlaw ladies
Sing until you scream.
Sing of all them raven-haired beauties,
The ones of whom we dream.
Then tell of the gen-u-wine queen of hades,
Belle Starr the bandit queen.

Now the audience realized they'd been had. There was no "SCOUTS OF THE PRAIRIE, a smash Broadway Extravaganza in Four Acts, Featuring the Biggest Names of the New York Stage!" as the exorbitant subscription contract, lavish handouts and front-door playbill had promised.

There was just a drunken ex-Indian fighter with a bad voice.

The violence now reached cyclonic proportions. Someone sneaked into the kitchen and came back with several dozen fresh eggs that were sent flying.

Even above the din, Cody could hear Dunn's screams: "Cody, I'll have your ass. As God is my witness, I'll have your bloody balls. You'll pay for this or I'll have you behind bars. For the rest of your days."

Cody leaped behind the old upright with the piano man, took a deep breath and looked for exits.

Angry patrons were vaulting onto the stage. Screams of "CASTRATE THE BASTARD!" and "SWING 'EM HIGH!" echoed through the saloon.

Cody's eyes darted back and forth frantically.

In another second, the irate, defrauded mob would be on him and his ass would be grass. Or, even worse, tar.

Then he saw it. Behind the stage, off to the left, a window opened on the alley.

A patron spotted him behind the piano. "THERE HE IS! CRUCIFY THE SONOFABITCH!"

Cody muttered a short prayer. God, please, not tar and feathers.

He helped himself to one last drink and heaved the Jack Daniel's through the window. Charging across the stage amid breaking eggs, flying bottles and the double booms of the sheriff's 8-gauge Greener, he dived through twenty-six pounds of Cincinnati window glass and vanished into the night.

19

For a long time Cody lay in the dark.

And dreamed.

He dreamed of men he'd known in the War. Men like Bill Hickok, George Custer and Little Phil Sheridan. He dreamed of the other side too—those who'd tried to bury him. He dreamed of the rebs he'd fought, and the Indians too—Yellow Hand whom he'd killed and Sitting Bull whom he'd come to revere.

But mostly he dreamed not of war and glory, nor of gold and girls; he dreamed of horseshit.

In fact, when he came to, he lay facedown on the bottom of a stall. His face was buried in the straw, sawdust and manure.

Slowly, with excruciating weariness, Cody rolled onto his back. And looked up. Painfully he propped himself on his elbows. Above him stood a huge hammer-headed bay, thick-shouldered and slab-muscled.

As he stared at the animal, the big mount lowered his long ewe-neck. He studied Cody with sad eyes.

"You can't hurt no worse'n me," said Cody.

Which was undoubtedly correct. Cody's stomach burned venomously and the pain in his head was starting to soar.

He didn't feel one bit better when he heard an eerie, grating *crack*! The stall door opened, and standing in front of him were Dunn and Sheriff Wilson with Lawyer Hargrove and Father Tibbs close behind.

"Anyone home?" Lawyer Hargrove asked.

"How'd you get in here?" Cody said.

"Through the keyhole like the Tooth Fairy."

"How do you feel?" asked Tibbs.

"The hair hurts."

"He smells like a manure spreader," Dunn noted.

Cody glared at him with a hostile bloodshot eye.

"Man who looks and smells as good as you must do real fine with the ladies," Sheriff Wilson observed.

Slowly, gingerly, Cody rubbed the back of his neck. "How did I get here?"

"After bustin' through the saloon window," Sheriff Wilson said, "you sloped on down the alley. I figured you for a lowlife scum-suckin' horse thief, so I guessed you'd go where the best horses are. I sent one of my deputies to the stable."

"What makes you so sure I was stealin' a horse?" Cody asked, his memory dimmed by the pounding in his skull.

"That's *my* horse we caught you in the stall with. That was *my* saddle you was slippin' onto him. That was *my* dep what stopped you."

"How'd he do it? With a howitzer?"

"He hit you with the manure shovel."

Lawyer Hargrove brought out a leather-encased brandy flask. "Uh, gentlemen, I think Mr. Cody might see things more clearly if we allowed him a touch of the hairy dog."

"Better let me check it first. Some men'll poison a horse thief." Sheriff Wilson helped himself to a snort, then handed it to Cody.

Father Tibbs stepped forward to stop him. "Not so fast, Sheriff. Is it wise to tempt a sick man's soul with the evils of drink?"

Wilson shrugged. "His soul's your job, Sky Pilot. I just want his neck."

"My son," the priest said to Cody, "I hope you have accepted Christ Jesus as your Savior?"

"If he's bankrolling that bottle, I sure have."

"Aw, hell," Dunn said, "give it to him. Cody weren't never worth sewer-piss drunk, but he's always been worse sober."

Sheriff Wilson handed Cody the flask.

Cody unscrewed the cap and took a stiff pull.

He was working on another when Wilson took back the flask.

"And now, Cody, we have before us the small matter of your finances."

"Yeah?" Cody said grimly, still eyeballing the brandy.

"Let's see," Dunn said, going over a column of figures. "When your acting troupe failed to show, you were expected to reimburse me over eleven hundred dollars in subscription receipts. Which you were unable to do. When you then insisted on drunkenly attempting to put on the show yourself, and in the process provoked the riot, you became responsible for over five thousand eight hundred dollars in damages. Throw in nine hundred and fifty-five dollars worth of hotel bills, the fines Sheriff Wilson will impose on you—including the attempt to steal his horse. Well, you start to see the extent of your financial problems."

Cody's eyes were bleak.

"Now, what puzzles us," Sheriff Wilson said, "is that these two men have offered you a way out. All you have to do is go with them, and they'll pay us off. But you won't follow them to *Mejico*. Why?"

"I got a thing about tacos."

"You're gettin' to be a true pain in the dick," Dunn said.

"A real hard-on," Wilson agreed.

"I can be difficult," Cody agreed.

"That's a hand we call and raise."

"Meanin'?"

"Meanin' we got a whole jail full of people you provoked. Held for being drunk and disorderly, malicious destruction of property, beatin' the mortal shit out of friends and neighbors. Meanin' you have bought them good ole boys a whole jailhouse full of grief. So when I lock your sorry ass up with these malefactors, they're gonna have a field day."

Sheriff Wilson looked down on him like a man who has just drawn a cinch hand.

"Cody," Dunn said, "they're gonna squash your sombrero."

Lawyer Hargrove returned the flask, and Cody helped himself to another drink. He looked up at the four men, his eyes haggard and bloodshot.

"Friend," Lawyer Hargrove said, "this is not a life I would choose."

"Maybe I hear a different drummer."

"Does he know how to drum 'Taps'?"

"There're some things I don't do," Cody said stubbornly. "Like *Mejico*."

"Our records indicate that you've done just about everything else," Lawyer Hargrove said. "You've shilled for snake-oil shows in San Antone. You've peddled poisoned whiskey to Indians in the Badlands. You ran a string of syphilitic hookers in Sante Fe and you panhandled in Dodge. We know you sold your saddle in Tascosa, and you're now about to eat county food in Abilene."

"So I'm a whore." He shrugged.

"I'd take their offer, boy," the sheriff said. "Before your breath comes in rattlin' gasps."

"I need another drink," Cody said.

Hargrove handed him the flask.

Cody upended it, and didn't quit till he was sucking air.

"Damn, he don't even stop to catch his breath," said Dunn.

Cody held the inverted flask over his head and looked up into its empty depths.

Father Tibbs broke in. "Mr. Sutherland's instructions were quite adamant in regard to Torn Slater. He felt he wronged the poor man most egregiously and wished to make amends. Slater has been guaranteed legal immunity, and we understand you know how to contact him."

Cody searched through his shirt pocket and dug out the butt end of a brown quirly. He scratched a lucifer with his thumbnail and lit it.

"What makes you think Slater would show?"

"The usual reason," Lawyer Hargrove answered. "Money."

"Filthy lucre does have its uses." Cody nodded.

"I would be curious to meet Mr. Slater," Father Tibbs said.

"He leads a rather stimulating life," Cody agreed. "He has a certain destructive capability, you know?"

"I'm more interested in the state of his soul."

Cody broke up.

The laughter rapidly dissolved into a fit of coughing.

"What was so funny?" Father Tibbs asked.

"I never heard no one suggest Torn Slater had a soul before."

"The sands of God's love are running out on you," said Father Tibbs. "I would strongly reconsider Mexico."

"I sure don't have many friends down there."

"Got any here?" Wilson asked.

Cody fixed him with a close stare.

Wilson had eyes of a hydrophobic rat.

"Cody, what do you know about the territorial prison in Yuma?" Wilson asked.

"It's a jail. It's in Yuma."

"When we finish with you in Abilene four or five years from now, I could arrange for you to spend your good-time down there. They chain you to the cell floor, nights."

Cody looked up at Lawyer Hargrove. "Try Calamity Jane. She's got a house of joy on one of them Rio Grande islands near El Paso. If she can't find Slater, no one can."

"We tried her. It didn't work. We'd like you to take us to Slater," said Hargrove.

"He won't wanna see me. He don't like me."

"First good thing I've heard about him."

Cody struggled to promote a grin.

Father Tibbs reached into his cassock and produced a small hand mirror. He handed it to Cody.

"I had the stable boy get this from down the street. Have a look at yourself."

Cody glanced into the mirror.

And shuddered.

"Tell me," Father Tibbs said, "do you really wish to go through life looking like this?"

"Why waste your time?" Wilson said irritably. "This gent's finished. Look at him. Horse thief, whoremonger, bald-faced liar, deadbeat and hopeless drunk."

Still staring into the mirror, Cody said, "You'd draw conclusions on such little evidence?"

Hargrove took a folded picture from his pocket.

It was a portrait of Cody in the midst of a pitched Indian battle. He was young, handsome, vigorous, in a fringed buckskin jacket, mounted on a huge, deep-chested white charger. His long sandy hair was blowing in the wind while, all around, scores of soldiers fought valiant Indian braves.

His fist, high overhead, wafted the bloody scalp of Chief Yellow Hand.

Underneath the portrait the inscription read: *Son of Morning*.

Hargrove returned the mirror to Cody.

In one hand, Cody held his life's prime.

In the other hand, hell.

"Bill," Hargrove said, "you were a good man once. To find that man again, you have to return to *Mejico*."

Cody stared at the two portraits, his eyes dimmed with tears.

Hargrove fixed Cody with a hard stare. "Let's face it. You have no place else to go."

PART V

I've read some of those pathetic penny-dreadfuls you vomit up each month. You are really
quite loathsome, you know. Is there no sewer
so foul that you will not slop around in it?
—Jacqueline Hardy to Ned Buntline,*
    Wild West impresario and author of
    557 dime novels

*Ned Buntline was the pen name for Edward Z. C. Judson. He is
often cited as the father of the paperback Western, and some of
the events in this book are adapted from his colorful and flamboy-
ant life.

20

Ned Buntline sat on the edge of his hotel bed. He was wearing his best tweed suit; and his large, square ruddy-complected face sported a perpetual grin. He knew he wasn't the handsomest man who ever courted a girl. His nose looked like a badly busted knuckle, and he was fifty now—a hard-used, bottle-worn fifty—but still he gave it his best.

The object of his desire was worth it. There, in one of the newfangled Morris chairs—the kind that tilted back as the arms were raised—was a small, beautiful, almost waiflike woman. Her waist-length yellow-gold hair was carefully coiled over her left shoulder. Her large eyes, blue as God's own heaven, were wide and expressive. Her pert nose, pouty bee-stung lips and fetching smile radiated unstained innocence. She was, to Buntline's jaded eyes, breathlessly beautiful.

"Allow me to pour you another drink, my dear,"

Buntline said, smiling. On the mahogany sidebar were a bottle of Dom Perignon and a half-full liter of Four Star Hennesey. Grabbing both of them, he turned to his friend. He poured a healthy double shot of cognac into her massive crystal goblet and topped it off with the champagne.

Her fifth double jolt of the last hour.

He refilled his own glass on the bedside table, replaced the bottle on the sidebar and resumed his vigil on the bed.

As the young lady sipped her drink, Buntline paused to admire her pale blue satin dress. He gazed longingly at the gossamer-sheer fabric, carefully swagged at the hip; at the daring neckline; at the soft, sensual upper garment so cunningly form-fitted around the breasts.

She appeared to have nothing save two lacy black stockings underneath.

"Tell me, Mr. Buntline, what was your military rank during the Rebellion?" she said, breaking the silence.

"I was brevetted colonel at Cold Harbor for valor."

"That's a lie, Private Buntline. My husband and I were friends with the late General Custer. He often remarked that you had entered as a private, made sergeant and then were broken back down to boot. 'For cowardice in the face of the enemy, misuse of government funds, illicit enticement of officers' wives and three hundred and thirty-seven counts of public drunkenness' was the way the late general described it."

"Ma'am, since you brought it up, yes, the late general and I had our differences."

"I can see why. I've read some of those pathetic

penny-dreadfuls you vomit up each month. You are really quite loathsome, you know? There is apparently no sewer so foul that you will not slop around in it."

"My dear," Buntline said smoothly, "I am deeply hurt that you disapprove of my books. However, I am an author, and I must write what is in my heart, what I feel."

"You must not feel very well."

She belted back another slug of brandy-and-champagne, staring at him over the rim of her glass with contemptuous, unblinking eyes.

"Jacqueline, dear, if you only understood the pain of being a writer. It is such an unbearably lonely profession. If you only knew how much I yearn for a woman of your taste and refinement. If I could only—"

"Get off it, Buntline. Are you suggesting your intentions are actually honorable?"

"Mrs. Hardy!"

"Well then, why have you brought me up here? And why have you pumped me full of these ridiculously powerful boilermakers? Why, each time you gape at my legs and breasts, do you have to slaver?"

"I had hoped to know you better. Perhaps let you read my work-in-progress."

"Mr. Buntline, I am told you compose these three-hundred-page books in three days."

"I know it sounds impressive," he said modestly.

"Not at all. They read like it. They read like they were written with pneumatic drills, which apparently they were. Your novels are trash, and you, sir, are a hopeless, boorish hack."

"If you got to know me better, I'm sure you would—"

"—*loathe you*. Sir, I am a woman of artistic temperament, forced into the role of the bored, long-suffering wife. And you are a fourth-rate, lowlife publishing whore. What are you doing even as we speak? Plying me with drink, exploiting my ennui, circling like a blood-crazed carrion bird, all in hopes of hammering me senseless on that bed."

"Please, Miss Hardy. It was never my intention to—"

"Oh, stow it, Buntline. Don't talk to me as though I were stupid. You didn't invite me up here to talk about the loneliness of a pulp-scribbling, ink-stained drunk. Nor was it to lecture me on art-for-art's-sake. You saw me as just another honey, one more of your sexually abused, drink-besotted dollies, something you could quickly finish off and then be on your way."

"You fail to take into account my heightened sensibility, the infinite esteem in which I hold the feminine gender. I have always—"

"Can it, Buntline."

Jacqueline Hardy tossed back her drink in one prodigious gulp. She rose from her seat, eyes blazing.

"Tell me, you simpering piece of weak-kneed chickenshit, did you really think I would fall for something as insultingly sleazy as *this*?"

"Most of them do," Buntline said with an embarrassed nod.

"Have you no shame at all?" Jacqueline growled. "God Himself graved the words: 'Thou shalt not commit adultery.' Moses warned us that 'the man who committeth adultery with another man's wife, surely that adulterer shall be put to death.' Is that the fate you wish for me?"

Buntline sheepishly lowered his eyes.

He nodded his head once.

Twice.

"You wish me to fornicate with you on the bed? You wish me to return home stained with sin, flushed with shame? You would hang on me the Scarlet Letter that dare not speak its name? Mr. Buntline, what you are proposing is not a quick piece of ass but a lurid masterwork of sadistic horror."

"Not even one little tiny—?"

"Sir, do you even know the *meaning* of the word 'adultery'?"

"It has something to do with being an adult?"

Her disgust was exquisite. "This pointless farce has come to an end."

Even Ned Buntline knew when he was beaten. He rose drunkenly to his feet.

"Miss Hardy, you may find me in the bar downstairs. If you need any assistance getting home, I shall, of course, arrange for it."

He rounded the bed and entered the vestibule. Just as he reached the door, he heard a familiar *whisk-whisk-whisk-whisk* in the bedroom.

He paused, and he shook his head, trying to clear it. It couldn't be. He swore he heard a woman disrobing.

He returned to the bedroom. There stood Jacqueline Hardy, her dress lying in a heap around her feet.

"Mr. Buntline, it's clear you have no soul to lose. Still, there is the problem of your troubled flesh."

Buntline was slack-jawed with shock.

"Don't just stand there looking stupid, natural as that state may be. Get back in here."

"My dear, I would never do anything to compromise your flawless and untarnished feminin—"

"Get real, Buntline," Jacqueline Hardy snarled. "The only thing comes out of this sad-assed Lone Star State are steers and queers. Let's hope you aren't one of 'em."

"You surely don't mean that—"

"I sure do. A Texas man, hell, he ain't nothin' but a wetback makin' tracks to Topeka. So let's see if you got somethin' below your belt, 'sides bullshit, booze and penny-dreadful paperbacks."

With a pull of a drawstring, the corset separated and dropped to her feet with the discarded dress and undergarments.

Revealing two sumptuous breasts; a flat, sunken belly; a round, firm bottom; and a stunning triangular patch of gold-blond hair. And shapely tapered legs, so long they seemed to start at her shoulders.

Buntline charged across the room. With a yelp, he was free of his coat and shirt. He kicked off boots, sailed his hat across the ceiling and whipped off his belt.

Ned Buntline—author, actor and Wild-West impresario—was about to get laid.

21

Buntline lay with the Hardy woman in the darkened room on the big feather tick. It seemed as if he drifted in space—doomed, deranged, delirious. He was lost in a universe of tingling limbs and trembling delectations.

He was dizzy with satiation.

Before meeting Jacqueline, Buntline's view of sex had been that the man climbed into the rack, blew out his tubes, then climbed out.

"Get on, get in, get off" had been his oft-quoted philosophy.

But in two short hours, Jacqueline Hardy had flown him to places he'd never dreamed of. In fact, the entire room seemed to spin with her furious energy. Her very skin—so soft, velvety and translucent—radiated power. At times, it almost seemed to crackle. The air around her ripped and snapped and popped. As though she were charged with lightning.

By now he had balled her every which way but loose—up, down, all around. Still, above his furious protests, she went at him once more—till his fourth firestorm of hell-blazing lust exploded out of him with volcanic violence.

Then, just as he was about to throw her off, he was stopped cold.

An ear-splitting shotgun blast shattered the window and covered the floor with broken glass.

"Come on down, you loose-legged cheatin' slut!" a man shouted, barely audible above a mob's din. "You too, Buntline. You're dead fuckin' meat. Deader'n Abe Lincoln's nuts."

And to Buntline's horror, Jacqueline Hardy—oblivious to the violence and danger—was whaling on his hammer again.

22

Quickly, Buntline threw her off.

He jumped out of the bed and hopped around the room, pulling on pants, belt and boots. Next, he threw on his shirt and jacket; and slinging the money belt over his shoulder, he shouted:

"Who the hell are those people?"

Jacqueline peered out the side of the window.

"Half the town is down there with ropes, torches, tar and shotguns. And there's my husband. He's back from Austin. He was supposed to be there the rest of the week with his business."

"What the hell was he doing there?"

"He and his partner run the Bull's Pizzle, a few other saloons and, I've heard, several rather unsavory establishments."

"You said the Bull's Pizzle?"

Buntline was a frozen tableau of horror.

"Why do you ask?" she said, still glancing over the window's edge.

"Uh, his partner wouldn't be Ben Thompson? Bloody Ben Thompson? The one who's killed more men than Hickok and Wes Hardin put together?"

"In fact, they do call him Bloody Ben sometimes. He seems to like it."

Suddenly, the mob got louder. A big man in a black suit shouted over the din, "Don't worry, Buntline. We ain't gonna just lynch you. We're gonna try you fair and square, then lynch you."

A drover in a wide-brimmed Stetson yelled, "You're goin' down by inches, Buntline. A loose noose and short drop. We're gonna take our time puttin' you under."

Buntline stared at Jacqueline and gulped hard. "You sure his partner's Ben Thompson?"

"I ought to know. He's also my lover."

Buntline's jaw dropped. "You mean I've been screwin' Ben Thompson's mistress?"

"YOU MEAN HE'S BEEN SCREWIN' *MY* MISTRESS?" Ben Thompson echoed from the hallway.

"Oh, shi-i-i-i-ttt," Buntline groaned, making the second word five long syllables. "You got a judge 'round here can get me out of this?"

"My husband's the judge."

She and Buntline quickly pushed the sidebar and bed in front of the locked vestibule door.

."What about the sheriff?"

"Thompson's the sheriff."

Thompson emptied his revolver into the door, and a second round of shotgun blasts splintered the front wall.

Buntline grabbed the pull-rope from the ceiling

fire escape. Yanking it down, he gathered up the three coal-oil lamps and slung their wire handles over his right arm. He started up the fire escape ladder nailed into the outside of the escape's trapdoor.

As he headed up the ladder, Jacqueline shouted above the din, "What do you want the lamps for?"

"It's dark up there," Buntline yelled back as he reached the roof and pulled up the trap. "I may need some light."

23

Buntline crouched low along the hotel's shake roof. The Sweetwater main street ran a good quarter mile, and to the north, by Buntline's reckoning, he had a half-dozen rooftops as an escape route.

To the south he had only one—the Lone Star Saloon. He decided to head north, but first he needed a diversion.

The Lone Star Saloon was a floor shorter than the Imperial Hotel's six stories. Buntline, keeping low, dropped the first coal-oil lamp onto the rooftop, where it shattered.

Shielding a lucifer with cupped hands and holding it close to the building, he flipped the blazing match onto the Lone Star's roof.

Sweetwater lay in the Staked Plains, one of the hottest, driest spots in the Southwest. The buildings were all baked dry by the scorching sun, and when the match hit the coal oil—half of which had slopped down a ventiliation shaft—the saloon's roof and top story almost exploded.

Now the mob shouted, "FIRE! IN THE LONE STAR!"

Buntline—bent low to avoid silhouetting himself against the night sky—gazed up the long line of rooftops to the north.

He hoped he could make six of them.

As a bucket brigade formed to put out the Lone Star fire, he dog-trotted north, two coal-oil lamps still dangling from his elbow.

24

Buntline used both lamps to torch the Sweetwater Hall of Justice, two rooftops north of the Imperial. He did this not only because he found the deed poetically just, he had other reasons. All of which were purely practical.

The Hall had a broad stairwell directly below the roof. Someone had thoughtfully left a sprawling pile of shingles there—all of which he promptly doused with coal oil and ignited.

Now Buntline was hauling ass. The next rooftop over—the Ace High Drinking and Pleasure Emporium—was flush against the fourth floor of the Hall, thirty feet straight down. And while his leap was boldly picturesque, the roof was so warped and cracked that he almost broke through to the floor below.

In fact, his right boot did penetrate, provoking high-pitched shrieks from three stark-naked daughters of joy piled atop a bare-assed man in a thick black beard and matching wool socks.

Another time, Buntline would have laughed uproariously and saved the scene for one of his novels.

Not now.

A searing blast of white-hot agony shot through his right ankle. He had either broken it or set a new track-and-field record for torn ligaments.

Moreover, his boot was trapped in the wreckage. One of the whores leaped off the bed, grabbed onto the swollen, twisted instep and hung there for dear life, wailing like a banshee.

Buntline's agony was exquisite. A mob wanted his neck. A bitch wanted his balls. His ankle screamed at him like all the tormented souls in hell. The fire was spreading to the Ace High where he was caught like a beaver in a bear trap.

He fought to get loose. Inch by crucifying inch, he wrenched on the pain-racked joint. Even as slat and shingle groaned; even as harlot mightily hung on; even as he choked and gasped on black, billowing smoke.

At last, with a horrifying sob, he tore the ankle loose. It was barefoot—minus the handsome, lavishly stitched Wellington boot of black British calfskin, half of the pair which Buntline had had custom-made in Brighton Rock two months before for $2,800.00.

But this was no time to mourn. As Buntline crept to the edge of the roof, he could hear all three whores—now hanging stark naked out the brothel's top window—shouting to the firefighting mob below:

"Help! Up here!"

"Stop him! Stop the bloody bastard!"

"Your man! He's gettin' away!"

Still, Buntline sneaked a peek into the street. He was glad he did. Despite the hysterical women hanging from the window, despite their bare flopping breasts and windblown hair, despite their flailing arms and frantic shouts, his fiery diversion had worked. The mob was otherwise occupied.

Over a hundred scurrying people had gathered to fight the fire. Drovers, miners, storekeepers, soiled doves, bankers, lawyers, stable hands and drifters—all were joined in common cause to put out the conflagration.

Three freighters—their teams blindfolded with grain sacks—had collected every bucket, hand basin, wash-tub and empty coal-oil can in town. They passed them in a long, twisting queue from the train station cistern to the burning buildings, where the firefighters ran them upstairs or sluiced down the adjacent buildings.

Whenever one of the bucket-passers paused to stare at the shooting flames, his face shone with blinding light.

He could tell by their eyes he was free.

No one gave a rat's ass for the screaming hookers. They had a town to save.

25

It was only when Buntline turned north along the rooftops and the first round ripped through his shoulder, that he knew how much trouble he was in.

Looking back, there they were, standing amid the flames of the Imperial Hotel roof: Ben Thompson and Frank T. Hardy—Jacqueline's husband—armed with Winchesters.

Buntline took off along the rooftops at a slow, limping trot. He stayed bent at the waist to give them a smaller target, while the bullets whistled past his ears.

The rooftop alongside the Ace High was only a one-story drop; but the way Buntline's ankle was ballooning, he didn't know whether he could survive the fall. He glanced back. Thompson and Hardy had traversed the first two roofs and were negotiating the two-story drop from the flame-shrouded Hall of Justice onto the Ace High.

Buntline allowed himself a small smile. It was a thirty-foot drop onto the busted roof; and if that didn't turn them back, nothing would.

To his horror, Thompson went over the edge of the Hall, and Hardy followed a heartbeat later.

Now there was nothing for it but to haul ass. While those two were digging themselves out of the roof's wreckage, Buntline had to make his escape, even if it meant limping off on *two* busted ankles.

He took a deep breath, and held it.

He went over the edge.

Buntline hit the roof of the Sweetwater Savings and Trust on a roll. Coming to his feet, his right ankle felt as though a grenade had exploded inside it—but he still kept his balance. He took off across the bank just as hard as he could hobble. The other two were also on their feet and charging after him, only two buildings away. Again, bullets were whistling, whining and smacking around him.

He was so stunned by pain and dread that he almost went over the edge. Arms flailing, skidding on his busted ankle, he ground to an agonizing halt.

Tottering at the brink, helpless, sick with vertigo, he peered over the edge and gasped. The street was three stories straight down. There was no way he could make the jump without smashing his ankle to a pain-racked pulp.

He turned to face Thompson and Hardy. They were civilized white men. Once he explained the extenuating circumstances, they'd understand. He threw his arms up and shouted:

"I surrender! I give up! You can take me in! I admit it! I admit everything! I fucked up!"

The heavy .44 slug from Thompson's Winchester kicked him in the right arm, spinning him to the left.

Which was the only thing that saved him.

Hardy's round was sighted in right between his eyes, but since he was knocked off center, it glanced off his temple.

Knocking him over the building's edge, thirty feet to the street below.

Into the bloody grace of black oblivion.

26

Buntline hadn't noticed the green awning on the way down—partly because it was dark out, partly because Hardy's glancing bullet had sent him over the roof backwards. In fact, when he hit the heavy canvas—flat on his back at full spread-eagle—he was so stunned by the rifle slug, he was only vaguely aware of passing through it.

He didn't really come to until he hit the open hearse beneath the awning. He found himself lying on his back atop a deep oak coffin while two men frantically struggled to pull up the black canvas sides and top. One man was an aristocratic-looking gent in an undertaker's suit; the other a priest in a jet cowl with a large silver crucifix around the neck. They both worked furiously, as if they had been expecting him.

As soon as the top and sides were up, the two men rolled him off the coffin and opened the lid. Inside, on a heavy white winding sheet, a soldier was laid out in dress uniform. They lifted the corpse out of the coffin by his shoulders and feet, grabbed Buntline the same way and lifted him into the empty box.

"No," he gasped, "don't."

"Get used to it, sport" the aristocratic-looking gent said. "Prison will not do much for your highly refined mind."

"It didn't before," Buntline agreed.

"What did it teach you?" the priest asked.

"How to break rocks, braid horse halters, clean latrines."

"Well, don't worry. These men won't send you back," Lawyer Hargrove said. "They cling to the cult of violence. They will kill you."

Buntline lifted himself groggily on his elbows and peeked over the casket's rim. The two men were lifting up the soldier by the ends of the winding sheet and preparing to place him on top of Buntline.

"Oh shit," Buntline groaned.

"Control yourself, boy," the aristocrat said. "We're about to slip some rotten meat in there to make the coffin smell like cholera. If they come into the hearse or open the lid, you have to keep quiet. Otherwise, it's all our hides."

He saw the soldier lifted overhead, then lowered on top of him. Following the trooper came the foulest piece of maggoty meat he'd ever smelled. It was shoved under the winding sheet, just below his armpit.

As the coffin lid was shut and locked, he heard Thompson and Hardy banging on the hearse door.

27

The voices outside the coffin came to Buntline as faint and far away.

"What do you mean, he's not here?" Thompson was shouting. "I shot him two, maybe three times. I saw him go over the edge of the building. Any fool can see the hole in the awning. What're you sayin'? You sayin' he sprouted wings and flew away?"

Beyond the casket Buntline could hear the muted din of the mob gathering around the hearse.

"Gentlemen, gentlemen," the good Father was saying, "all I know is that we have the remains of an innocent soldier who succumbed to cholera during the epidemic at Fort Bliss. As a favor to the family, we have agreed to haul him back to Kansas."

"Father, I don't care what you say, there ain't but one place where that rascal Buntline could be hid. Somehow I gotta think he's in that coffin."

"The good Father said cholera," Lawyer Hargrove reminded.

"I'm still gettin' a look in that box," Thompson said.

Buntline heard a murmur of approval from the mob, then the canvas sides and top being rolled back, then the lid latches clicking open.

Slowly, his eyes squinted shut, he heard the lid being lifted.

As the foul stench of the turning meat hit the crowd, the hearse exploded with screams and wails.

He felt the crash of the slammed lid.

With a gasp, Buntline passed out cold.

28

The next night, they stopped to make camp. Buntline had been out of the coffin for most of the day, but he was still queasy. He squatted before the fire, unable to eat food but trying to keep down some coffee.

"Tell me," Father Tibbs said, stirring the embers with a piñon stick, "how do you see yourself? The patron-bard of Wild West barbarism?"

"That's a pretty good line, Father," Buntline said wryly. "Maybe I'll use it in my next novel."

"Let's face it, Buntline," Lawyer Hargrove said, "you're not really a writer. You're a parasite and a predator. You survive by victimizing others, not by literary endeavor."

"Anything wrong with that?"

Father Tibbs glanced at Hargrove, still stirring the fire. "I find his attitudes starkly Darwinian and a profound embarrassment to the Holy Mother Church."

"Yes," Lawyer Hargrove agreed, "I'm heartily sick of his foul-mouthed bravado. I'd really like to return him to that Sweetwater mob."

"Thompson would know how to handle him," Father Tibbs agreed.

"Wouldn't it be pleasant to see Buntline after Thompson got him—all cocky and exuberant one moment, dead the next."

"Hey come on. You guys talk about me like I was something you get from a bait shop."

"Let's face it, Mr. Buntline. You are not exactly in great demand as a citizen. There aren't too many towns around here begging you to take up residence."

"Hey, give me a break," Buntline said self-pityingly. "I've been through a lot lately."

"Aw, have you now, ducks?" Hargrove said sarcastically. "What would you like me to do? Chuck you under the chin and look pathetic?"

"You two make me feel like something stuffed by a taxidermist and mounted on a wall."

"Really, Mr. Buntline, you do yourself too much credit. But how about something from the reptile cage? Or a medium-size water rat?"

"Look, I don't care what you say. I didn't just roll in on the back of a turnip wagon. Me and Sutherland go back a long way. You think he's laying any scratch on me, think again."

"You scared?" Lawyer Hargrove asked with amusement.

"A man messes with Sutherland, he has to be brave or insane. I'm neither."

"Mr. Buntline," Father Tibbs said patiently, "Sutherland is dead."

"Which means nothing. I know him. He's capable

of yanking that stake from his heart, clawing his way out of the grave, zooming down to *Mejico* on a broomstick and biting the shit out of my neck. I know the bastard."

"But you're perfectly safe now. Mr. Sutherland wrote that will in his own hand."

"Just words. Just paper."

"Trusting soul, aren't you?" said Hargrove.

"Yeah?" Buntline said. "Give me one good reason why I should go down."

"Mr. Buntline," Lawyer Hargrove said, "I am not a God-fearing man. In fact, I subscribe to the gospel of violence. You want a good reason for not going down to Mexico? Let's try violent death."

"I said a *good* reason."

"Believe me, I did not risk my hide saving you from that mob to let you foolishly run off. We will have our colleagues take you to the old *monasterio* in irons if need be. Or back to Sweetwater. The choice is yours."

"I still don't like it."

"Then give us the names of your relatives," Hargrove said. "We'll tell them you died in surgery."

"This is not my day," Buntline said gloomily.

"You have to learn hope, my son," Father Tibbs said. "Hopelessness in the Holy Mother Church is the only unforgivable sin."

"I got shut of that hope shit years ago," said Buntline.

"Please, Mr. Buntline, you have to be more optimistic."

"All of us do," Lawyer Hargrove agreed.

"Men in our line of work," Father Tibbs said, "we always need optimism."

Buntline shook his head sadly.

He watched in dismay as the cross-hobbled mule team cropped the grass under the hearse's axle springs.

He was heartily sorry he'd balled Hardy's wife.

PART VI

We are all in the belly of the beast.
He is in us, and we are in him.

—Father Tibbs

29

The countess sat in her palatial hotel suite at the Delmonico Hotel in Denver. In the light of an overhead scroll-pattern crystal chandelier, she stared at the triptych mirrors of her Louis Quinze cherrywood dresser.

In the three mirrors, the splendid furnishings of the Delmonico were lavishly reflected. The massive brass bed with its fringed spread of red shantung silk, the heavy teak drawing table with its narrow high-backed armchairs, the vast hearth-blackened fieldstone fireplace with the handsome reproduction of Rembrandt's *The Blinding of Samson* above the mantel. The ceiling molding glistened with gilt, and on the marble-topped mahogany bedside table a sterling silver vase contained one perfect red rose.

Slowly, she focused on her own reflection. She decided she looked a good ten years younger than her thirty-six. As if to confirm this generous self-appraisal, she let her powder-blue satin dressing gown fall open.

She began a careful, critical self-examination.

She started with the shapely, tapered legs; followed them up—all thirty-five and one-eighth inches up—from the soles of her feet to the rich roan-hued triangular bush over her *mons veneris*. She continued up—up, up, up, up to the hard smoothness of her flat stomach. She threw open her gown the rest of the way, the better to scrutinize the spread legs and sumptuous breasts with their pert upturned nipples and wide pink aureolae.

She commenced a meticulous inspection up the slender throat, searching for wrinkles—which thank God!—were still years in the future. She smiled, and when the smile reached the wide-set violet eyes, she was pleased.

She took a deep breath and let it out slowly, saving the best for last: the great cascading mass of honey-red waist-length hair, which regardless of fad or fashion, she wore long. Staring into the mirror, she realized once again that if she had any real claim to serious beauty, it was these stunning Titian-hued tresses. They framed the milky skin, the wide-set eyes, the sultry mouth, the pert nose and made them all glow.

At least, she hoped they did. Tonight she needed every edge. Tonight, her beauty would have to launch fleets, foment wars and burn the topless towers of Ilium.

Slowly, with cold calculation she ran the brush through her long, auburn locks.

30

"Well, ducks, you look dressed fit to kill. Right-o? All set for another night of wonder and revelation?"

The countess was still sitting in front of the mirror, putting the finishing touches on her makeup and evening wear. Gorgeously gowned in a lavender dress of pongee silk, her pouty, artfully bowed mouth garish with lip rouge, she felt like an exotic, richly perfumed flower.

"Wonder and fornication, you mean," the countess said dryly.

Lord Worthington threw his head back and laughed merrily. "Glad you haven't lost your delicious sense of humor, old girl. Tonight could prove to be downright hilarious."

"Screamingly funny."

"Utterly uproarious."

The countess—no more a peeress than Lord Worthington was a lord—shot her partner-in-con a curious sideways glance. Duded up in a slate-gray tweed suit with a floral pattern brocade vest, a bowler of matching gray, a handsome shirt of white raw silk and a black bow tie, he did manage to look like English royalty. Particularly with that 20-karat gold-rimmed monocle jammed into his eye.

Only a bleeding count would dare to wear a ruddy monocle, as Worthie was fond of saying.

Lord Worthington jabbed the air with his ebony walking stick, the one with the sterling silver winged-eagle handle.

"My God, you're a vision of breathtaking loveliness."

"What about the war paint?"

"A little heavy on the lip rouge and mascara, perhaps. After all, we don't want you looking like a tropical fish, do we?"

"Arthur's partial to the embalmer look," Lady Cynthia said with a shrug.

"It was ever thus."

The countess sat back negligently, crossed her legs and sighed. "Well, there she is. Burnished to a high gloss."

"Yes, my carnivorous little viper, you are a dream. And don't think our Arthur won't appreciate it. Just thinking of all those luscious loins and vast Venusian mounds, why, he'll be pissing sweat from every pore. Between your wondrous charms and his astonishingly suicidal greed, he doesn't have a prayer. You'll have him bent over the bed with his pockets pulled out before he can even say, 'How much?'"

"That's what I love about you. Your teary-eyed sentimentality."

"Yes, I have a big heart. It's a failing of mine."

"Yeah? Well, suppose he's not as stupid as you think."

"Could it be otherwise? The poor lad loves you uncritically. You've shackled his soul and snared his heart. You have him by the ruddy balls."

"You talk about him like he just fell off a hay wagon. I'm not so sure."

"You keep your pretty face buried in his lap, and he'll be too dizzy to suspect."

"You really think he's that simpleminded?"

"He's an unfunctional idiot—one-half greed, the other half dumb desire. You sell him the phony gold mine, give him the old razzle-dazzle, and we'll be on the midnight train to Canada with a suitcase full of gold certificates before he knows what ran over him."

"The poor unsuspecting fool. I've never had one so pathetically lovesick before."

"Think of him as one who loved not wisely but too well."

She fixed Worthington with a hard stare. His mouth was grinning brightly, but the eyes were flat and cold as a diamondback's. She always knew Percy was heartless. They had been running cons together for almost twenty-two years, since she was fifteen years old. But at moments like these—just before they took off the mark, and she stared into Percy's glassy, expressionless eyes—it was as though she'd never known him at all.

"He'll be coming up any time now. You'd better be leaving. You might spoil the mood."

He turned toward the door, then stopped. "Save your pity for those who deserve it. You're a bleeding countess, and he's had a royal ride. He'll never again know anything so thrilling."

Percy left.

The countess sighed and stared into the mirror. Something was wrong. Always she'd lived without doubt, scruple or hesitation. She'd plunged shrewdly and remorselessly through life. But now she felt as if the passion had lost its charge, the salt its savor.

What was it that bothered her?

Perhaps it was the rat of guilt gnawing at her conscience?

Or was something wrong with the con?

She still could not believe Arthur was *that* stupid.

31

Arthur and the countess stared at each other across the drawing room table. For the occasion, they had ordered four broiled lobsters, two pots of drawn butter and three silver ice buckets chilling magnums of Monopole.

Cynthia even managed a look of genuine love-longing, which wasn't easy. Arthur was no ravishing specimen of rugged frontier manhood. He was a stockily built, highly successful wheat farmer from Iowa with a sunburned nape crimson as the countess's broiled lobster.

Still, she managed a sigh of passionate rapture. She gazed fondly into his heavily freckled moon-shaped face, his pale gray eyes, his bulbous nose and dumb-hick grin. She forced her eyes to pass over the boiled shirt, celluloid collar and the store-bought frock coat of coarse black wool.

She tried instead to focus on the fact that this was

a man who owned 13,600 acres of prime Iowa farm-
land and was looking for investments.

She concentrated hard on the cashier's check for
$193,000 which he had in his brown leather money
belt tightly circumscribing his bulging belly.

Slowly, her gaze, her smoked, dreamy eyes and her
wide, expansive grin grew more luminous, more
ecstatic.

"Arthur," she asked gently, "you never talk about
your late wife. Is it too painful?"

"She was a good woman, an excellent mother," he
said with a bland shrug, "but nothing like you."

"I'm sure she was a wonderful person."

"She was decent enough, but, like myself, out of
touch with her feelings." His eyes looked goggly
behind his thick-lensed glasses.

"But Arthur, you're so generous and affectionate.
She must have loved you very much. She must have
been terribly special."

"She dismissed feelings as lust. My impulses, well,
she saw them as degrading, perverted."

"Oh, Arthur, that can't be true. You're so open, so
giving."

Arthur smiled abjectly. "She couldn't handle my
desires."

For a long, awkward moment they were silent. The
countess pretended to play with a piece of lobster
claw, cracking it open with great effort, then sucking
on a piece of the tender meat inside.

She made a great display of it.

"I love you so much," he whimpered, choking with
emotion.

She put the lobster down in a display of haste.
"Oh, let's get the other things done. Let's get the

deed and that silly quit-claim signed so we can get on with your feelings, your impulses and desires. Oh, my darling, we both have so much to learn about each other. I believe tonight is going to be so very special. Once we start, I don't want to stop for anything."

Arthur's briefcase was at the foot of the bed, and he quickly had the quit-claim, the deed and the $193,000 cashier's check out. She sat on the edge of the bed and looked them over.

"Now, countess," he said solemnly, "are you sure you want to go ahead with the quit-claim? Our marriage will cost you your title; and once you give that up, you will be just a commoner. Like myself."

"Then I shall love you as a commoner," she said, gazing into his pale eyes.

She quickly signed the quit-claim.

"And the deed. The old mine meant a lot to your family. Are you sure it's wise to give me half of everything?"

"Oh darling, the family doesn't need the money. And anyway, you're putting up a hundred and ninety three thousand in venture capital. You'll be the one financing the drilling operation, the turbine pumps, the smelting plants and refining mills. You'll be the one meeting the payrolls once we hit the mother lode."

"But, dear, the assayist's report virtually guaranteed eight hundred dollars to the ton, and that was on the alluvial ore alone. Once we hit the big veins, why, it'll be another Comstock."

"Oh Arthur," she said, her eyes brimming with tears, "I don't care about the silly money. All I want is you."

He took her hand and squeezed it warmly. "One day you may think I did this for the money."

"Never, my darling, never."

She promptly released his grip and signed the deed over to him. Now she stared at the certified cashier's check from the Denver Mint.

$193,000.

Big Casino.

"Can you really cash this tonight? My brother is so intent on starting immediately."

"The faster he starts, the faster we hit paydirt."

She watched him breathlessly as he handed her the check.

"Now you endorse it, and I will be right back with the cash. Five-hundred-dollar gold certificates, just as Lord Worthington asked. And then we can consummate our engagement?"

"A consummation devoutly to be wished," she said in a throaty whisper.

In the doorway, they kissed; then he was gone.

Slowly the countess turned to the mirror. She looked at herself a long, long time. She wanted to pinch herself. It couldn't be true. This was the biggest scam she'd ever run.

"One hundred and ninety-three big ones," she whispered to her reflection conspiratorially. "One hundred and ninety-three thousand dollars."

32

It was just as she had started to repeat "One hundred and ninety-three thousand dollars" that she heard the knock on the door.

"Let me in," Percy Worthington growled.

Irritably, she opened the door.

He entered with a distinguished-looking gentleman in an expensively tailored dark suit, and a priest in a black cambric cowl. The two gents looked solemn as royal hangmen. Worthington looked white as a sun-bleached buffalo skull.

"Let's move it," he said bluntly, "They're closing in."

"What?" she said, incredulous.

"The feds are on to us. The con's blown."

She glanced into the eyes of the gentleman and the priest. The gentleman's eyes were hard and flat as a timber rattler's; and the priest, while polite, seemed ready to perform Last Rites.

She suspected he was always ready to perform Last Rites.

"You better move it girl," the tall man said tonelessly.

"Who are you?" she asked, grabbing her prepacked emergency "traveling bag" from a closet.

"Lawyer Hargrove and Father Tibbs. We're here on behalf of the late James Sutherland. You two have been named in his will. Unfortunately, we have also learned from some helpful feds that they're about to bust you for a phony gold-mine fraud. Since our first obligation is to the Sutherland estate, we're prepared to smuggle you out of town."

"How?"

"Through the services of a friendly funeral director. The transport is just outside. The rest you really don't want to know."

Her face was a stunned mask of disappointment and disbelief. "Where are we going?"

"To the Mexican desert."

"I hate the desert. I hate Mexico."

"Think of its primitive beauty."

"Anyone who goes to Mexico for its primitive beauty would go to hell for the nightlife," she said.

"Move it or lose it," Percy said, glancing hurriedly at his watch.

Lawyer Hargrove glanced out the window.

"We better take the rear exit. Here comes Arthur with a squad of dark suits."

"Not Arthur," she groaned.

"He's the best bunko man north of the Medicine Line. They borrowed him especially for you two."

"You blew it all on a fed," Percy said with genuine commiseration.

"Father," Cynthia said sadly to Tibbs, "what must you think of us?"

Father Tibbs's eyes were mercifully expressionless.

"We are all in the belly of the beast," he said. "He is in us, and we are in him."

"The important thing now," Percy said, "is to make tracks."

They were out the door, rushing toward the back stairs.

"Lord Worthington tells me you two are actually married," Father Tibbs said pleasantly. "So many young people these days sleep together without the sanctity of sacrament. I'm so glad you two aren't like that."

The countess glanced at him, incredulous.

"Do you two like marriage?" Father Tibbs asked as they hurried down the steps.

"The first two years were the best," Percy said.

"Really?" Father Tibbs asked.

"No doubt," Lawyer Hargrove explained caustically. "Our records show he spent them in Andersonville."

They were silent the rest of the way down the steps.

PART VII

I have no use for trash. Men who gouge and desecrate the sacred earth, men who violate the belly of the Holy Mountains for useless sand and worthless rocks, such as these, the gods do not forgive. These fools shall crawl through the afterworld forever. As moles.
—Geronimo

33

The Apache chief called *Gokhlayeh,* or "He Who Yawns," by fellow Chiricauhuas—and baptized "Geronimo" by his implacable white enemies—was showing signs of restlessness. "Volcanic violence" was the way Indian agent Tiffany described it.

Ever since his breakout from the San Carlos reservation—followed by a score of murderous raids into Mexico—he had been bored. And upon his return to the San Carlos compound, his boredom had turned bloody. As a result, the Chiricauhua agent, J. C. Tiffany, had jailed him five different times.

The first instance was in February. Geronimo had knifed a brave named Little Ears over a gambling debt. The wound had been superficial. Little Ears had not only refused to press charges, he had promptly paid back the debt, and Geronimo had therefore

135

argued that his week in the guardhouse was both unjust and unjustifiable.

The second charge, from Geronimo's point of view, was more serious. He had caught one of Agent Tiffany's representatives cheating the Chiricauhuas on agency beef. A cattleman named Graves had driven a diseased, stringy herd of two hundred range steers up from Chihuahua. They were little more than bones, parchment and festering insect bites by the time they reached San Carlos. So Graves had salted them up, then turned them loose in the San Simon River to bloat.

The cows quaffed over thirty pounds of river water apiece, which as soon as they stepped off the scales, they voided onto the reservation stockyard ground. And as Geronimo and his Chiricauhuas stood there watching—and smelling—the steers piss their winter rations into the stock corral, he went berserk.

Graves, he tried to kill.

Tiffany, he attempted to castrate and dismember.

For which crimes he got two months in jail.

By the time Geronimo got out, it was July; and the brown, windowless adobe guardhouse with its mud-and-mesquite roof was hot as a hell-furnace. Furthermore, Geronimo left jail with a sense of smoldering outrage. Not only had he served half the summer in a superheated sweatbox, he knew that the Chiricauhuas would spend the winter starving.

Adding insult to injury, this time he learned that one of his wives had cuckolded him with the shaman. In a moment of jealous wrath, he cut off his wife's nose and took off after the shaman with a shotgun.

He was captured by the reservation police before further harm was done, but even so, it was fall before the next jail sentence had been served. When he got out, the first thing "He Who Yawns" did was to finish his shooting of the shaman. Since the shaman survived, Geronimo's crime was not irredeemably heinous. Apache jurisprudence, like white-eyes justice, allowed adulterized husbands a certain understandable leniency.

However, in this instance the charges were aggravated. The shaman insisted Geronimo had shot him not in protest of his wife's loose morals, but because of a bill he owed the medicine man.

Among the Apaches, failure to pay the shaman was the most serious offense on the books. The Chiricauhua Apaches were intensely religious people with a fanatical fear of the afterworld. As a consequence, the tribal shaman was held in high esteem. Only the shaman, with his charms and spells, could save men from this hellish afterlife. Those who antagonized the medicine man were cursed on earth and wandered the Dead Land eternally.

As ghosts.

So once more "He Who Yawns" found himself in lock-up.

This time facing a long, long stretch.

34

It was late November when Geronimo got a visit from Snake Woman. Since the death of Ghost Owl, she had spent her time as a translator for the white-eyes. Now she stood outside the guardhouse waiting for Geronimo to be released.

The two of them were not friendly, and he glared at her disdainfully. The old woman was dressed in typical Apache garb, a mid-length doeskin dress and a top that extended well below the hips with a yellow lightning bolt blazoned on the back. The seams were double fringed, with numerous sacred cords, bags and sashes festooned from her neck and waist. The entire outfit—including her thigh-high rawhide-sole moccasins with the turned-up toes—was heavily beaded. Her graying hair she stubbornly wore in the fashion of a man—straight and shoulder-length with a concho-studded buckskin headband. A sheathed trade knife hung from a belt, which gleamed with conchos and brass tacks.

Geronimo studied Snake Woman's face with scorn. It was brown as an old hide, fifty years of crow's-feet etched into the corners of the eyes. Then he sneered gloatingly at the harsh scars. Twenty seasons past, they had been lovers, until in a jealous frenzy Geronimo had slashed her cheek and nose. The first cut crudely traversed her right cheek; the second ripped through the left side of her nose.

Slowly, his twisted sneer crooked into a frown, and Geronimo's eyes narrowed. He remembered what happened after he cut her. Her new lover had beaten him mercilessly. He could still see the insane tormentor towering over him—the broad blocklike shoulders; the huge, heavily veined biceps; and the astonishingly narrow waist. He remembered the man glaring down at him as the blood-guttered black-snake whip rose and fell, rose and fell. The brave's eyes had been terrible. They were the hardest, blackest eyes he'd every seen, flatter than a diamondback's, flatter than a snapping turtle's. And even more pitiless.

With a crawling, shameful shudder, he remembered blubbering like a child—sobbing and pleading for mercy. Mercy from his rival and blood brother. From the one the Chiricauhuas called "Blood Ant."

The one the white-eyes called Torn Slater.

The frown deepened as Geronimo studied his shabby attire. It wasn't much. Dirty buckskin leggings. Shabby thigh-length moccasins. His massive chest was nut-brown, bare-naked, streaked with dirt and sweat. His dark, hawk face was heavily lined. He looked exactly like the thing he was: a hard-used Apache convict.

As he stood there—eyes blinking and squinting in the brilliant sunlight—he glanced over at the two Apache guards. They were armed with Winchesters and Peacemakers and were standing a dozen feet away. Behind them were two white men clad in black. One, a tall, angular serious gent. The other, a black-robe.

"I am pleased to say you look terrible," said Snake Woman. "It is obvious that jail doesn't agree with you."

"I should not have stopped with slashing your nose," Geronimo said tonelessly. "I should have cut your cackling throat."

"*Enju.*" Agreed. "And perhaps then the *pindah,*" the white man, "your rival, would not have stopped with flogging you bloody. Even after you whimpered for mercy like a whipped child. Perhaps Blood Ant would have beaten you to death."

Geronimo frowned and looked away. "Have you come only to jeer an old enemy? Or do you now work for the *pindah lickoyee*?" He nodded toward the two white-eyes.

"They come seeking your release from prison. An old enemy of ours, the white-eyes they called *Suth-er-land* has died. He lost his mind toward the end and wishes to leave you some of the yellow metal."

"I have no use for trash. Men who gouge and desecrate the sacred earth, men who violate the belly of the Holy Mountains for useless sand and worthless rocks, people such as these, the White-Painted-Lady, the Child-of-the-Water and the Holy Gans do not forgive. Those fools shall crawl through the afterworld forever. As moles."

"Is there nothing you seek from the white-eyes?"

"I would take their many-shot rifles. The weapons you load today and shoot all week. With enough of these, we could leave the white-eyes' reservation and hold off the palefaces forever."

"With the yellow metal you could buy the many-shot rifles."

Geronimo crossed his arms and arrogantly averted his eyes.

He considered this woman's opinions beneath contempt.

"Don't strain your simple head. If you want the rifles, go with these men. Accept their yellow metal. Otherwise, you will remain in jail. Hopefully forever. Those are the alternatives."

"Do I face this ordeal alone? Is this a trap?"

"No, the white-eyes named Cody is going. So is Blood Ant."

"Blood Ant is going?"

"Enju." Yes.

"What do you believe?"

"That they will have you murdered. You remember how our people were tricked into going into Camp Grant and were massacred. The same with Carasca in *Mejico*. Cochise and Mangas Coloradas tried to meet with the white-eyes. Both were trapped and nearly killed. The governors of Sonora, Chihuahua, Arizona and New Mexico have us hunted for the money on our scalps."

"Are you sure this meeting is a trick?"

"I am sure it will be violent and dangerous."

"But you also believe Blood Ant will be there?"

"Enju."

"Good. We shall tell the jailers that Geronimo is

through with the guardhouse. This journey to the mountains is just the thing I need."

"I do not believe you will survive it."

"Then it is a good day to die. This will be the perfect trip to whip me into shape. It will prepare my weary soul for our Battle-to-the-Death-with-the-White-Eyes."

"Then go with God, as the *Mejicano* pigs say."

"And with the devil, you babbling, scar-faced old hag." Geronimo glowered at her venomously.

She returned his glare with equal hate.

Finally he wheeled around and swaggered up to the two black-clad white-eyes, arrogantly swinging his arms.

Geronimo was going to war.

Geronimo, alias *Gokhlayeh,* alias "He Who Yawns," was grinning.

PART VIII

Sitting Bull knew that what awaited his people was a horror too great for even the stoutest heart to endure. In Sitting Bull's True-Vision, he saw the Sioux nation as a small nail and the white-eyes' army as a vast hammer. This was a curse beyond horror and tears, a living-waking nightmare in which death lurked not only in the heart and soul but in the shadowland where Sitting Bull's ancestors and descendants would now wander eternally. In this vision the Sioux nation's sacred land was a dark and bloody ground and the people no longer blessed by Wakan Tanka but forever damned, forever accursed.

—Sitting Bull's True-Vision

35

Sitting Bull was old.

As he sat in his teepee, puffing on the ceremonial pipe, it showed. His massive square face, weathered as the Dakota hills, was burned nut-brown. When he smiled, frowned or clenched the calumet tightly in his teeth, his face was furrowed by an infinite maze of deeply etched wrinkles. Staring into the smoldering fire, he shivered, pulled the buffalo robe tight around his cold, weary bones.

Even though it was a temperate spring, he could not seem to get warm. The long, brooding winter had blown through his soul like a black wind, and though the teepee was thick and well-aged and the inside of the buffalo hides heavily blackened by the smoke of countless fires gone, Bull still grumbled of the cold.

In truth, there was no reason for it. Bull was revered. Among the white-eyes he was regarded as an historic figure, and among the Sioux virtually a god. All his needs were looked after. The floor of his lodge was covered with deerskins. A heavy bearskin hung over the crawl-hole. The lavish array of weapons and gear attested to his wealth: colorful buckskin blankets and buffalo robes, horsehair halters, countless three-foot cane arrows fletched with vulture feathers and decorated with red and black bands. Two double-bent bows of oak and mulberry painted black with yellow lightning bolts zigzagging the twin curves. Wrist quirts, saddlebags, quivers, and bow covers of mountain lion skin with the fur and the tails still on, adorned with sun signs and the wheel of life. Several trade knives, a double-barrel shotgun, two repeating Winchesters, a half dozen Colt revolvers, a bow drill, flints and pyrite. By the Sioux standards, Bull was a wealthy man.

Still, sitting in the warm lodge, he shivered. Moreover, Bull knew this bone-deep chill had nothing to do with an inclement spring or the rigors of age.

The Sioux were in trouble.

Bull was in trouble.

And he needed a vision.

It was toward dusk that Bull told Fire Eyes to bring on the stones.

36

Bull had always loved things old—customs as well as
possessions—and one of the advantages of his ancient,
smoke-blackened buffalo hide teepee was that it lent
itself to the holy ritual of the sweat bath. The hides
were so caked with soot that they trapped the heat
perfectly. So when his niece, Fire Eyes, fetched him
the hot white rocks, spread them around the fire
and poured gourdfuls of water onto them, the lodge
was quickly filled with steam.

Bull ordered more and more rocks. As Fire Eyes
brought in the smooth white stones, the lodge grew
unbearable with the steam. By midnight Fire Eyes
could only tolerate the temperature for minutes at a
time. Her face and hands were blistered.

Still, Bull signaled for more rocks. Perhaps it was
his age, perhaps the conditioning of a lifetime, but
his skin remained unscorched by the heat. Higher

and higher the hot rocks piled and steamed. Hotter and hotter the teepee grew.

On and on, Bull's thoughts drifted.

Into the night.

Into the past.

Into the void.

37

Mostly, Bull thought of the Greasy Grass. It had been the Sioux's most stirring moment. Not only had Bull rallied to unite all thirteen bands of the Sioux nation, he had talked the Cheyenne, the Arapaho and Gros Ventres into joining. Crazy Horse, Rain-in-the-Face, Gall, Hump, Fast Bull, Crow King and Black Moon led these violent tribes and had served Bull well.

Together, they had given the white-eyes the worst drubbing in the history of their many Indian wars, first at the Rosebud and then at Greasy Grass—later called by the white-eyes, Little Bighorn.

How often had that encounter haunted him? After the Rosebud, the prospect of such a battle had filled Bull with dreams of darkness and dread, and on the day of the climactic fight, Bull had vowed to sacrifice the scarlet blanket, the far-famed sun dance.

Even now, he recalled with astonishing clarity striding to the holy tree, sitting before it, leaning back against the trunk and beginning the trilling wails, imploring the gods for a sacred vision.

Then the immolation. It seemed fitting that his adopted brother, Jumping Bull, assist. When Jumping Bull had been eleven years old, Sitting Bull had massacred his family during a battle. However, Bull had been so impressed with the youth's courage in the face of certain death that he spared him. Now at Bull's finest hour, at the moment of his supreme vision-quest, Jumping Bull was to perform the rite.

With a needle-pointed awl in one hand and a sharp knife in the other, Jumping Bull knelt beside his brother-through-choice. He cut into Sitting Bull's right wrist. Piercing the skin with the awl and lifting the skin, he sliced it off with the knife. Jumping Bull, then, moved up the arm swiftly, precisely. Stab, lift, slice. He made fifty slashes from wrist to shoulder, after which Jumping Bull turned to the left arm and performed fifty more cuts.

Not once during the sacrifice did Sitting Bull flinch or falter in his singsong trilling wail. He sat there motionless as stone, blood covering his arms, dripping from his fingers.

This was Wakan Tanka's—"the Great Mysterious One's"—scarlet blanket.

Sitting Bull recalled how he had risen from the sacred tree. He had stood, glazed eyes fixed on the sun, bouncing up and down on his toes, rhythmically. Chanting and praying and singing his monotonous tremolos, he stared at the sun all morning and afternoon. He danced without water or sustenance, through the night and all the following morning.

When the sun was at zenith, Sitting Bull had collapsed, unconscious.

And slowly his vision came: An army of bluecoats emerged from a drifting fog, heads hanging in defeat, hatless, broken, doomed.

Wakan Tanka—"The Great Mysterious One"—was offering Sitting Bull victory.

Slowly Sitting Bull sat up. Leaning against the sacred tree, he said to those gathered around him, "These soldiers coming into our valley are gifts of Wakan Tanka. Kill them." But then Sitting Bull added, "Do not take their guns or horses. If you set your hearts upon the white man's goods, it will prove a curse to this nation."

So the battle was joined in the valley of the Little Bighorn. The troops of the white-eyes against Sitting Bull's army of four thousand Sioux, Cheyenne, Arapaho and Gros Ventres. Crazy Horse, Rain-in-the-Face, Gall, Hump, Fast Bull, Crow King and Black Moon had led these nations like a blaze of lightning bolts. By dusk, Custer and his brothers, Miles Keogh, Lonesome Charlie Reynolds, and every other man in Custer's battalion lay facedown in the dust of the Little Bighorn Valley—mutilated, murdered and robbed.

Oh, the warriors had proclaimed it a holy day, a great day, and had praised Wakan Tanka for his gift. Sitting Bull had chanted and war-danced and trilled the singsong kill-tales with the rest.

But his heart was leaden. His vision had been leached. One day his people would pay. He knew it in his soul.

The impact of Sitting Bull's vision was felt instantly. The greatest Indian army on the continent quickly fell apart. Sitting Bull and his Hunkpapa Sioux fled to Canada. There, for four years he and his people lived in hunger and privation; and when he returned to his land, Bull entered the white-eyes jail.

Still, he knew the worst was yet to come, and for all his life Sitting Bull chanted and sacrificed, sun-danced and prayed for another vision—for guidance, for the wisdom to lift the curse which he knew Wakan Tanka had placed on his people. All the suffering and death his people had endured would be as nothing when compared to the enormity of Wakan Tanka's wrath.

Others had denied truth. Young seers had risen with dreams of the buffalo's return and the revival of the great chiefs, with splendid visions of the day the warring tribes would reunite and the Great Sioux Nation would retake the land. Sitting Bull would nod slowly, smoke the ceremonial pipe and encourage his people in these hopes and dreams.

But, in truth, Sitting Bull knew that what awaited his people was a horror too great for even the stoutest heart to endure. In Sitting Bull's True-Vision, he saw the Sioux nation as a small nail and the white-eyes army as a vast hammer. This was a curse beyond horror and tears, a living-waking nightmare in which death lurked not only in the heart and the soul but in the Shadowland where Sitting Bull's people, ancestors and descendants, would now wander eternally. In this vision the Sioux nation's sacred land was now a dark and bloody ground and the people no longer blessed by Wakan Tanka but forever damned, forever accursed.

Unless Sitting Bull could find a way out.

An escape from the downward sweep of the swinging hammer.

A secret egress from eternal damnation, and the hopeless hell of what their Comanche brothers called the Land-Between-the-Winds.

38

It was dawn. Sitting Bull had sweated in his lodge since dusk, smoking the ceremonial pipe, praying and chanting for a vision which would bring peace.

But whose peace? Do you seek the peace of your people or do you merely wish to calm your own troubled soul and ease your own restless heart?

Years before, *Hunka Wambli,* or Spirit-Eagle, the one the white-eyes called Torn Slater, had told him of an ancient white man called *O-dys-seus.* This man had been a great warrior who was forced by the gods to wander a vast body of water for ten-and-eight seasons. He had faced horrible giants, evil witches and terrible storms. Still, the lust for adventure burned in him like fire, and after a brief reunion with his wife and child and a short stay in his homeland, he yearned again to roam the seas. "To follow honor like a sinking star" was the way *Hunka Wambli* had phrased it.

Sitting Bull asked *Hunka Wambli* how the great warrior stilled his hunger for travel, battles and adventure, knowing that he had never found this secret key to easing his own unquiet soul.

Hunka Wambli had replied that the ancient warrior, on the advice of a blind shaman, had shouldered his oar, trudged to a high holy hill far from the sea and buried it deep in the sacred soil.

That night Sitting Bull, unbeknownst to his tribe, had carried his war lance far into the Black Hills and plunged it into the sacred heart of the holy earth.

Still, unease plagued his sleep, and nightmares thrived.

He saw *Hunka Wambli* one last time. He asked him the question he had failed before to pose: Did the burial of the warrior's oar divert him from his quests?

No, *Hunka Wambli* responded.

What happened, then, to this *O-dys-seus*?

He rallied a group of old friends, and they went on one last voyage, *Hunka Wambli* replied. A long and dangerous yet strangely beautiful quest. And, while they all perished in the end, still they saw many wonderful things, performed great feats and they lived—and, more important, died—like men.

So that was that.

There at dawn in the scorching heat of his night-long sweat bath, it came to Sitting Bull what his True-Vision might be.

If he were strong enough and brave enough, he would atone for the sins of his people and his forebears. Oh, the journey would be hard. Bull had no doubts about that, and he would need a sacred band of holy *hunka*-brothers to support him on such a trek. But if he could find this hallowed host of blessed comrades, and if he could set out on a voyage like the ancient warrior *O-dys-seus,* he might be granted one more True-Vision by Wakan Tanka. This would be a vision capable of healing his nation's wounds, of uniting the broken and fragmented bands of the Great Sioux Nation, perhaps bringing back the vast herds of buffalo and pronghorn and mule deer and elk. This would be wondrous and a noble vision, grand enough to bring together all the Indian peoples everywhere and make them Brothers-through-Choice the way the Great White Father in Washington so glowingly announced they should be but Who, in fact, proceeded to steal their land, poison them with firewater and disease and herd them like convicts into prison camps.

Bull could do it. He could make his people whole. He knew he could. With a True-Vision.

With a sacred band of friends, with strength and courage and cunning, he could survive that arduous journey and atone in blood for the sins of his forebears, his descendants, for Indian peoples everywhere.

Bull prayed that he be granted such a vision.

Though he suffer it in blood.

And pay for it with his life.

39

When Bull left his sweat lodge the sun was at zenith.

He had had a wonderful dream.

He had seen himself surrounded by many *hunka*-friends—by Cody, Slater and Buntline. The Apache warrior the white-eyes called Geronimo and the Chiricauhuas called *Gokhlayeh,* he had been there too.

He knew that, on the journey, he would be granted his vision-quest.

Looking up, he saw a white-eyes in a frayed elkskin jacket. Even before his failing eyes focused, he knew who the man was. Cody. From his dream.

Two other palefaces stood beside him. A tall, somber man in dark garb; and a black-robe with a silver neck crucifix.

Tears of joy dimmed the old chief's eyes.

He strode purposefully across the campground.

Toward them.

PART IX

Eyes that burn like blazin' fire,
Lips that taste like honey-dew.
Mouth's a hot live lungin' wire,
Wayward, cunning, cruel.
She'll twist you in the heat of desire,
Till you're beaten, broken, through.
   —J. P. Paxton, "Belle Starr, the Bandit Queen"

40

Twilight in the Nations.

Five horsemen in dirty white dusters and sweat-stained Stetsons paused at the top of a low ridge. Squinting into the deepening dusk, they stared at the small spread below. A large long-billed wren perching on an overhead pine bough scolded them; and a dozen feet to their left, a striped Gila woodpecker picked a hole in a saguaro. A roadrunner darted past their horses and vanished into the chaparral.

Henry Morton Stanley stared down at Belle's ranch. The main residence was modest but trim. It was built of split red-hued logs, a shake roof and a fieldstone fireplace. A fenced-in Holstein with a full bag peacefully cropped a clump of bear grass, and the densely green backyard garden suggested an ample pantry—full of turnips, squash, onions and sweet potatoes.

The three huts out back were made of clay and

interwoven maguey stalks. The roofs were of sod, packed on a mesh of maguey and mesquite. Through the valley snaked a parched, shallow river, on both sides of which were scattered large patches of corn, beans and maguey. A barefoot Indian in a straw hat and a white muslin shirt tilled the bean field behind a span of mules. Stanley watched a funnel-shaped cloud of dust rise behind the plow, then settle and disappear. To the west of the main house was a stock corral full of saddle horses. Beyond the *remuda* grazed nearly a thousand head of cattle.

Immanuel Carpenter—the tall, angular rider with the brown hawk face, hooked nose and deeply etched lines around the eyes—motioned them down the slope toward the ranch.

Stanley fell in behind him. Deacon, the grizzled old trail hound followed. J. P. Paxton, the one in the black bowler, with the baby-fat face and the dark, flashing eyes, rode drag.

They leaned hard on their pommels, and entered a long, winding dry wash. Lolling in their saddles, they made their way down-slope, twisting and lurching to avoid the sharp-thorned mesquite, the pencil-thin, needle-pointed cholla, and the endless colonies of prickly pear.

41

They kicked their horses through the hock-high stream, and as they scrambled up the opposite bank, the ranch came alive. A score of Indians in buckskins, white peon garb and faded Levi's seemed to material- ize out of nowhere. They approached the horses, looking up at the riders with dead, expressionless eyes.

Their hands held axes, machetes and trade knives.

Stanley quickly caught up with Carpenter, anxiously filling the void. "What's Belle like?"

"What do you mean?"

"To talk to."

Deacon pulled up alongside them. "Ever try reasonin' with a spittin' panther?"

"Or try screwin' one?" added Carpenter.

"That mean she's bad in her boots or good in the sack?"

"Depends on the man. Cole Younger used to say

she was pure electric pleasure. Later he claimed she was more like a coiled-steel bear trap. But there she is now." Carpenter nodded toward the porch. "Figure it out yourself."

"Maybe I will." Stanley shrugged.

"Yeah?" said Carpenter. "Well, if you're gonna show some balls 'round here, just make sure you got balls to show. That bitch was born on the fast track."

"A real fire-eater, huh?"

"Mean enough to kill a rock."

They halted at the hitch rack in front of her porch.

42

All four men waited by the hitch rack. Carpenter threw a knee over his horn. Stanley, Deacon and the Professor leaned back in their saddles, waiting to be invited down.

Stanley studied Belle.

She was standing on the porch steps, her hips classically canted, an 8-gauge sawed-off on her shoulder. Her faded Levi's were tight across the crotch and ass. The black buckskin Stetson with the high horseman's crown had a diamondback hatband, the fangs and rattles still on. The hat was scoop-brimmed, badly battered, stained with sweat. It was a working Stetson, but she wore it at a rakish angle. Under the brim, Stanley glimpsed the slanting black eyes glinting with wickedness.

A double-lash wrist quirt with a leaded stock hung from her fist. She casually cracked the heavy rawhide plaits and the three-inch poppers against her knee-high boots.

Which were heeled with six-inch buzz-saw rowels.

Her black cotton blouse had mother-of-pearl buttons, the top three open to the navel.

Stanley stared and swallowed hard.

They were now surrounded by Indian workers armed with knives, axes and machetes, but she swept them away with an absentminded wave of the sawed-off.

"Professor. Carpenter. Deacon." Her voice had the quiet hiss of a diamondback buzz.

A warning rattle.

All three men touched their hats.

"This here's Henry Stanley," Carpenter said.

"Yeah. Know'd him from the picture papers. He's the reporter feller, the one what hung out with Hickok. What brings you here?"

"Lookin' for Torn Slater," Carpenter said. "The Professor says you were the last one we know who talked to him."

"What you want him for? You ain't lawin' for Judge Parker. Not with a squirt like the Professor along.

"Not likely. Slater's got a couple of friends what's in trouble. Think he'd like to know about it."

Belle shrugged.

She took the belly-buster off her shoulder and braced the butt-stock on her hip.

She continued to crack the boot with her double-plaited quirt.

"Yeah, maybe I seen him. Left a black pup with me six months back. Damn thing growed big as a year-ling steer. Mean enough to make you kick your gramma. Also saw him 'bout three weeks back. Tried to shuck some brass-knuckle Mex whore onto me. Claimed he wanted to reform her. Ain't that a pisser? Him reformin' a whore-lady?"

"Where is she?"

"Hell, she just 'bout crapped her pantaloons just thinkin' on the prospect. She shot it down faster'n I could."

"Any suggestions where we might locate him?" J. P. Paxton asked.

She stared back at them blankly.

"This is hard, hot land, Belle," said Stanley. "We rode a long way to find him."

She raked them up and down with dubious looks. "Ah, hell. You might as well come in. Sit a spell, have some grub."

"We'd purely 'preciate that, Belle," Carpenter said.

"Ain't much. I don't get many white men 'round these parts. Anyway, I 'spect I gotta hear what this is all about."

43

"Run that past me again," Belle said, her face incredulous.

The four of them sat around a large maple kitchen table. A soot-blackened pot of Arbuckle's rested in the middle. Alongside it was a jug of Old Crow. Stanley poured a healthy slug of bourbon into his cup and topped it off with more Arbuckle's.

"Back in New York after the Sutherland funeral, I started checking around. The whole thing struck me as, well, funny. So I made a few discreet inquiries at Lloyds of London, Bank of England, places where Sutherland had done extensive business. Nothing had changed. No insurance collected. No funds frozen. Financially, everything was business as usual. Even though he was dead. Something smelled."

"Your nose could have been wrong," Belle said.

"True, so I checked around some more. I came up with old Deacon here. Sutherland's head of security.

I found him in a bar. Drunk. He was still dressed in his black funeral suit and had been up for a week. He said he didn't know all the details, but that it involved Diaz and the McKillian woman. He also said Calamity and Cody were in trouble, deep trouble."

Belle's eyes were skeptical. "Cody and Clem in a bind?"

"And a bunch of others. A lawyer and a priest conned them all into going down there for the reading of Sutherland's will. Geronimo, Diaz, Sitting Bull, Buntline, the count and the countess. Slater was asked, but turned it down."

"He must have seen somethin' comin'," Carpenter said. "The only thing they're inheritin's an assful of trouble."

"You can't get word to them?"

"They're under private escort all the way," Stanley explained. "Incommunicado."

"So they've got them," Belle said.

"Not exactly," Deacon said. "Five or six good men could get in from the back, surprise those inside without alerting the Comanchero guard to the front."

Belle's silence was eloquent.

"What do you think?" Paxton finally asked.

"A mighty complicated way of killin' yourself."

"I checked it out," Carpenter said. "I know the old *monasterio*. It can be done."

"You hate Diaz so much," Belle sneered at him, "you'd charge hell with a glass of ice water if you thought he was there."

The Professor suddenly stood up, flustered. "My dear, my only concern is that we're wasting time. We have allies in the *monasterio* already. Cody, Bull, Buntline, Calamity, the rest. With those stout hearts, we'd be a dagger pointing straight at the heart of *Mejico*. We'd be an elite corps of shock troops, rivaling the Spartan few at Thermopylae. We would be—"

"You wanna take on Diaz and Sutherland," Belle Starr interrupted, "you better have something 'sides words. Them ole' boys cast a mighty long shadow south of that borderline."

"But our friends would help," Paxton persisted.

Belle laughed in his face.

"They're all seasoned veterans," Paxton argued.

"Bull's an old man," Belle sneered. "And Clem? If pussy was bullets, she could kill France. The count and his wife? They got more in common with Diaz and Sutherland than you three."

"You left out Mr. Cody," the Professor said. "He could do something to help."

"What Cody can do is about two quarts a day plus any woman who'll stand still long enough."

"What about Slater?" Stanley asked.

"I seen men with some hard bark on them," Belle said, "and Slater was the hardest. All he-coon and a mile wide. A real ramrod. And I don't mean ranch foreman neither."

"If this operation is so unsavory, why should Mr. Slater go along?" the Professor asked. "What would he get out of it?"

"His usual cut: grue, gore, torture and death. He'll find bitter foes and faithless friends."

"Why would he want to do it?" Stanley asked.

"He won't *want* to," Belle said. "He'll growl like a gut-shot grizzly. He won't understand why we can't get it fixed with fifty bucks and a fast-talkin' lawyer. He'll say it serves us all right and tell us to go fuck ourselves."

"What about yourself?" Stanley asked. "You have a nice spread. I don't suppose you could just take off?"

"Not hardly."

"Yes, Belle, my dear," Paxton said, "you've found your place in the sun at last. This spread is a dream come true, a golden season, a wondrous piping time of peace."

Belle stared at the three of them a hard moment, her eyes dark, expressionless. "You wanna know the truth? All this 'piping time of peace' and 'golden season' shit bores me. Maybe I ain't trackin' too well and maybe I spent too many years on them high lines. Maybe I had too many horses shot out from under me. Like a certain friend of ours south of the border. But anymore, I'm whip-dog tired. Wouldn't mind tryin' a real-life, down-and-dirty, no-shit desperado again. Just for a change. You wanna track down an outlaw? Pull your freight. Tell Slater that cartoon-strip dictator down there's got his girl. Cody and Bull too. Tell him it's root, hog or die. Jump or slide."

"You think he'll really come along?" Stanley asked.

"Sure. If we don't hold back the spurs or ask him nice. If we put it to him plain as the balls on a tall dog, ugly as a fart in church."

"It don't sound promisin'," Carpenter had to admit.

"Then you put the pistols on the table. Tell him these dudes down there got his friends, and he's their last best hope."

"I don't think he'll go for it," Stanley said.

"Then put the spurs to him," Belle said. "Tell him there's bullshit and showdown shit. And just make sure he knows the difference."

PART X

I ain't seen much worth laughin' at. Not since
Lincoln got his gruel from John Booth.
                                        —Outlaw Torn Slater.

44

Torn Slater was bored. Leaning back against the brass headboard, he reached behind his head and gripped the vertical struts with both hands. Like prison bars.

He glanced down at the woman's head dallying in his lap. Her lips wondered and whispered the length of his thighs. She strove with tender care to puzzle out the coy conundrums therein. She seemed so eager, so intent. She murmured honeyed, loving words; yearned to sweet-talk his vanished virility into a triumphant return and to reinflame the growling, groaning firestorm which had so recently ravaged both their loins.

He stared at her shiny black hair. He wished he could write off her ghost-walking lips and half-sobbed sighs as merely a whore's gambit.

But it was not so.

This was no ordinary *puta*. This was a truly primal

woman—a creature of gargantuan appetites, inexhaustible longings and almost criminally violent cravings. This was a woman who—after having racked him on that cantina cot for half the morning and most of the afternoon, after seven straight hours of endlessly crescendoing climaxes, maddening ecstasy and throaty, rasping, heartbreaking groans—had him beat.

Slater had to admit it: He was a stopped comet, a burnt-out volcano, a dead star. He could no longer satisfy her. He had just given her everything a man could possibly offer a woman. Everything except the one thing she now desired.

More.

Slater glanced to his left and caught his reflection in the wall mirror. His face was chalky white with exhaustion; his eyes hollow and sunken, consumed with dread. His pupils were dilated, the irises distant, turned in.

They were not even the eyes of a man but a ghost from hell.

45

Slowly Rozanna raised her head from his lap and fixed him with expressive, doelike eyes—black as anthracite, wide and sad as the grave.

"What is it, hombre? You no like me no more?"

Slater tried to ignore her, but the wet round tears rolled down her cheeks.

"Wasn't it no good, *guapa*?" Rabbit? she sobbed.

"Better'n bein' eaten 'live by hydrophobic termites."

"I know what it is. You no like your little Rozanna no more."

He tried to shrug it off, but her entire body was racked with sobs.

"I know you is tired of your Rozanna. You wanna go back to your gringo girl friends. Maybe that girl Calamity. First you steal my heart, then you kill my hombre Aquilar, and now you throw me out. *Ey?*"

He motioned her to be still, but to no avail.

"Look, amigo, if you no love me no more, I

unnerstan'. But you got to keep me in practice, no? For when you take me to *Mejico* City? After what you teach me, *madre mia*, we gonna make *muchos pesos,* yes?"

Amid her tears, she smiled bravely.

Torn Slater let it out between clenched teeth. "How many times I got to tell you? I ain't no pimp. I rob banks and trains. *That*'s my business."

"You tell me all businessmen is pimps."

"I ain't *that* kind of businessman." His voice was harsh.

Suddenly, she was in his arms. "I'm sorry, *muchacho*. I did not mean to insult your *machismo*. Jus' 'cause you no longer get it up, I—"

Slater froze, stopped dead by a hard rapping on the door.

"Amigo," the *patron* of the cantina said, "there are four gringos downstairs asking 'bout an *Americano* who sounds very similar to you."

"Saved by the bell," Slater said under his breath.

He stood up.

Eager to be out of the bed.

46

As Slater headed down the stairs, his eyes were alert to every movement in the cantina. He studied the dozen round tables with their quartets of bentwood chairs, filled with scores of Mexican and gringo customers in straw sombreros and felt Stetsons.

He stopped halfway down. He spotted four gringos at a corner table. Paxton, Carpenter—? Was that Hickok's friend Henry Stanley? And Belle Starr?

With Rozanna in tow, he continued down the steps and crossed the room. Reaching the front of the table, he pointed to Stanley, seated in the corner. "You got my seat."

Stanley rose, and Slater took the gunfighter's chair, back to the wall. He leaned deep into the corner, his right hand near the butt of his Colt.

"What you doin' 'round here?" Carpenter asked.

"Not much. Run a few tables. Bank. Buck the tiger. Keep out the tinhorns. See that the mescal ain't instantly poisonous. I take a two-bit rake-off from most of the pots."

"And sample the favors of every soiled dove here to Chihuahua," said Carpenter.

Slater looked annoyed.

Belle quickly added: "And no doubt leaves them a sight more soiled than he found them."

Slater was silent.

"Like pimpin'?" Belle asked.

Slater gave her a long stare. "It's a hard life. You gotta pay attention all the time."

"What kind of johns you get down here?" Belle pushed.

Slater met her gaze casually. "Men with more'n one name. Some more'n a dozen. Men who'll kill you for your boots—hell, for the heels. Or who'll rat you out to the *federales*."

"You recommend Nogales as a place to raise kids?" Belle asked.

"If your kids are Bill Hickok and Coleman Younger."

"How're the Mexican women?" Stanley asked. "I hear they're marvelous lovers."

"Starvation's a great aphrodisiac," Slater agreed.

"How's *your* girl?" Belle sneered.

"Nice kid."

"A little slow?" Belle asked, grinning.

"She was born with shiny black hair 'steada brains."

"Sounds just right for you," said Carpenter. He glanced at Belle. "Slater I knew, he hated to use a horse hard or a woman easy."

Slater glared at him.

"The Torn Slater I knew," Belle said, "when he

finished with a woman, she looked like something from a knacker's yard. Nothin' but remnants, dead meat and old bones."

"Belle, you could spend the summer at Doc Holliday's Dental Clinic up in Dodge." Slater's stare was hard enough to hurt.

"No, I wanna get this one straight. I wanna hear the big bad gringo gunman threaten a woman one more time. 'Specially seein' as how the only woman who ever meant a lick to him—meanin' Calamity Jane Cannary—'s 'bout to get herself raped, tortured and torn to pieces. I want to hear him threaten us womenfolk some more."

"Clem's down at the old *monasterio*," Slater said wearily, "and that ain't no problem. It's all cleared. I was even invited."

"You sure nuthin's wrong?" Belle warned.

"The only one means her any harm's Sutherland. And he's deader'n Abe Lincoln's nuts."

"Guess again, honcho."

She pointed to a grizzled old trail hound crossing the cantina toward their table.

"I got it from him. Sutherland's man. John Henry Deacon. You remember him?" Stanley asked.

"Yeah. He was Sutherland's chief of security or something."

"He can tell you all about it." Belle sneered. "For one thing, there's still Diaz. He's down there right now—bigger'n Beelzebub and howlin' for Clem's hide. He's waitin' to nail her and your friends right to the fuckin' floorboards. The only thing them heirs are gettin' from Sutherland's estate are the tortures of hell and a pine box. 'Less'n we can stop him."

"That's gospel," Deacon confirmed, pulling up a chair.

Slater gave a low whistle. "I hope somebody's got a plan."

Belle's grin was big as all Chihuahua. "Have we got a plan for you."

47

"That how the shit shines?" Slater said, after listening to the details of the rescue operation.

"That's the layout," Deacon said.

"That ain't no plan," Slater countered.

"Yeah? What'd you call it?"

"Some kinda horrible spasm."

The four stared at him somberly.

"Why not talk 'bout stealin' a ewe lamb from a wolf pack?" Slater asked.

"Or arm-wrestling a steak from a Great White?" Stanley grinned.

"Don't it shake you none?" Slater asked.

"Like the wind in the trees," Carpenter said.

"We don't pull this off, we're gonna end up lookin' mighty stupid."

"As well as mighty dead."

"You know this is a Temple of the Lord you're talkin' 'bout knockin' over?"

"More like a House of Assignation, the way they're planning to use it," Stanley said.

"Do they still stone people?" Slater asked.

"They do down here," Carpenter said glumly.

"It sure ain't the U.S. of A.," Belle agreed, glancing around the room with a shudder.

"I ain't even sure it's *Mejico*," Carpenter added.

"Well, what do you think?" Belle asked. "We ain't got all day."

"What's in it for me?" Slater said noncommittally.

"Clem's undying gratitude," said Paxton.

"Oh, I get it. You're sweet-talkin' me."

"What?" Paxton asked, confused.

"He wants us to appeal to his better instincts," Belle explained. "He wants us to offer him money."

The four stared at Slater with grim eyes.

Slater shrugged. "Suspect my woman'll have to come along. I ain't been able to shake her yet."

"You sure you want into this?" Carpenter asked.

Slater nodded. "Guess I figured I missed somethin', not gettin' to storm the walls of Monterrey with Zack Taylor and Bobby Lee."

"It won't be no barrel of laughs once we get there," Deacon pointed out.

"Who cares?" Slater said. "I ain't seen much worth laughin' at nohow. Not since Lincoln got his gruel from John Booth."

"Good show!" Stanley shouted.

The four comrades lifted their mescal glasses in salute, grinning enthusiastically. Slater raised his too while secretly, under the table, he massaged his battered groin.

With relief.

He was glad to be leaving Nogales.

48

The locomotive roaring through the *Mejicano llano* was a Baldwin eight-wheeler. It sported bright brass fittings, a voluminous cowcatcher and diamond-shaped, spark-spreading crownpiece billowing smoke and blazing embers. It was powerful enough to take forty ore cars up a steep mountain grade.

It pulled one tender and four lightweight Pullmans—two were sleepers, one a dining car, the other a double-size club car.

The guests quietly relaxed. Cody—a bottle of 1811 "Year of the Comet" cognac at his elbow, a full balloon snifter in his fist—sat with Buntline, Calamity, Geronimo and the countess and the count at a baize-covered poker table. They were playing seven-card stud for shares of their prospective fortunes.

Thus far, the big winner had been the countess. She was up $13,738.53, and the big loser was the drunken Cody—down nearly twice that.

Bull, disdaining both poker and plush armchairs, squatted in a corner of the car, rocking slowly on his heels. He smoked his medicine pipe, a long-stemmed, intricately carved calumet. His eyes were dim, distant, opaque. He was lost in trance.

At last, Buntline rose from the poker table. "Deal me out, friends." Picking up his brandy snifter, he turned to stroll the double-car.

Buntline had to admit that the accommodations were posh. They sat on plush bolted-down armchairs with thick Turkish carpets at their feet. Wall mirrors surrounded them, as well as broad observation windows. Between the windows and mirrors were hung exotic paintings of far-off lands: the rolling desert dunes of the Middle East, oases shaded with palm trees, and pyramids, harems, sultans, concubines with gaping navels and opulent breasts.

A half dozen stewards were setting out the dinner placings. The menu read duck *a l'orange,* and he assumed that it would be superb.

All the cuisine had been superb.

The only thing bothered him were the stewards—these six big *Mejicanos hombres,* two with noses broken more than once. Several had scarred, knuckle-popped hands, suggesting a life of violence rather than one of genteel stewardship. They all wore Colt .45's under their white linen serving jackets, and most also carried hideout pieces.

"Bronco bucks, they have jumped the reservation, no?" was the singularly terse explanation.

For a long moment Buntline studied the lavish club car.

The bolted-down tables were covered with snowy Irish linen. The settings were immaculate. The view was divine. Still, Buntline was uneasy. Something was wrong. Terribly wrong.

49

The accommodations for Slater and his friends were in no way lavish. The long sweaty ride in a sweltering boxcar filled with jostling *peons* took them as close as they could get to the foothills of the Sierra Madres. Next came half a day's bickering with a mule-trader, which was followed by shanks' mare and muleback through the broiling furnace-lands of the Sonoran steppe.

They were to enter the old *monasterio* by the back door. That meant a trek through blazing desert canyons, hazing a string of two dozen gelded jacks—the most cantankerous creatures on God's scorching earth—every inch of the way.

Before the first day was out, they were sunburned, butt-sore, boot-blistered, hateful of mules and just plain pissed. But they were on their way. Carpenter was up front, pulling jerkline; and Slater was in charge of loading the packs, which was an art unto itself. Flattening and smoothing the pack pads till they were flush and wrinkle-free. Balancing and rebalancing the loads over and over and over. Throwing the one-man diamond hitch and pulling the load together.

Slater labored over the packs with painstaking meticulous care while Paxton pondered the tense proceedings fearfully. Slater would haul on the lash rope; the load would wrench, jerk and strain; the kyacks, panniers and crossed wooden sawbucks would creak and groan. And Paxton would heave a tumultuous sigh of anxious relief each time Slater pulled the load together, threw the diamond hitch and tied it off.

Slater spent a good three hours packing each morning. They were transporting everything from knives to dynamite to rifles to extra shells to hand soap to pocket mirrors.

But mostly what he packed and repacked was water. Big five-gallon cans of it. Water which they cached under piles of scree in remote corners of the canyon for the trip back. Sutherland had hired a band of robbing, killing, scalp-hunting, white-slaving Comancheros to protect his front porch. The gang was headed by none other than Gentleman Jim Flynn, the most venomously hated renegade in two countries. This was a man to whom rape, torture and white slavery were a way of life.

If Flynn and those Comancheros came pounding up their back-trail, they'd need every edge they could get.

And in the Great Sonoran Desert, water was more than an edge.

It was survival itself.

50

The third day out, they rounded a bend. Slater scaled the canyon wall, and there he reconnoitered their destination: *Sierra de la Noche*. Mountain of Night.

At its summit was the old *monasterio*, and up through its bowels was a maddening labyrinth of ancient Aztec mine tunnels. Through these crumbling shafts and drifts; through the endless crevices and fissures; through the infamous *corredor de los murcielagos*, or cavern of bats; over the nightmarish guano pit and up the outside monastery wall, they would climb.

They had to breach the old *monasterio* and take Diaz's people by surprise. If not, there would be hell to pay.

For Sitting Bull, Cody, Buntline, the count and countess.

For Slater's brother-through-choice, *Gokhlayeh*, the one the white-eyes called Geronimo.

And for the only person on this sun-scorched earth whom Slater gave a damn about, the only person he would ever give a damn about.

Calamity Jane Cannery.

BOOK II

My friend, *Mejico* is a Catholic country, and we believe in redemption through pain. Without pain, there is no confession and expiation; hence, without it, we are doomed. I believe my people can still be saved. I shall save them. But most painfully, I am afraid.

—Porfirio Diaz, President of Mexico
from 1877 to 1910

PART XI

Romanticism is the deranged doctrine which falsely holds that love can overcome greed, power, hate, war and death. It is the dogma of a lunatic asylum. And believe me, these Romantics in *Mejico* get just what they deserve. Our penal mines and labor colonies cure them of all such misconceptions quickly and thoroughly.
—Porfirio Diaz, President of Mexico from 1877 to 1910

51

The old *monasterio* was erected by Dominican Friars in the seventeenth century. Its initial intent was fortification against Apaches. To that end, the first thing erected was the redoubt wall—thirty feet high, twelve feet thick.

Within this massive barricade, the old *monasterio* was slowly and meticulously erected. First its north and south transepts went up, then the colonnaded porticos opening into sprawling arcades, followed by the vast vault of the sanctuary soaring to echoing heights. Adorning the nave was every nuance of niche and grille, of alcove and carved screen. Soon, above it all, soared the supernal clerestory with its grand array of magnificent windows flooding the sanctuary with radiant light.

To build this stronghold, the mountains, hills and valleys had been stripped for fifty miles around. There was timber to be bucksawed into beams, corbels, door frames, panels, pews, furniture and window embrasures. A million tons of clay to be mixed with water and straw and molded into an infinity of adobe bricks. Every ounce of mica and selinite—for a radius of a hundred miles—to be melted and molded into the huge clerestory windowpanes.

There were thousands of tons of gypsum from rivers and streambeads to be powdered, mixed with water and gessoed onto the adobe walls till every square inch of brown earthen brick glistened white as snow.

And so the *monasterio antiguo* grew.

Murals, mosaics, sculptures in relief, illuminated tapestries, heavy altar draperies of damask and pongee. The central courtyard with its dazzling rose gardens, its sedulously sculpted shrubs, its endless rows of precisely planted, brilliantly blossoming cherry trees. A sprawling monks' dormitory, a spacious refectory, the lavish guest quarters upstairs, the library, wine cellar, hostelry, the farrier's forge and the vast stable.

But even so, the old *monasterio* never lost sight of its original intent. That of a refuge and redoubt. For underneath the sprawling splendor, it was nothing less than a fortification.

Its architectural plans were, in fact, a welter of labyrinths and secret chambers, murky passageways and hidden anterooms, vertiginous stairways and crumbling subterranean tunnels.

The old *monasterio*, a redoubt against the ungodly.

A safe haven for Dominican Fathers.

Righteous Soldiers of the Lord.

Founding fathers of the Holy Inquisition.

52

It was a grand group assembled in the refectory. As the twilit dusk filtered through the overhead stained-glass windows, bathing the room in a dazzling rainbow of blues and yellows and reds and greens, Calamity Jane could not get over how many people had turned out.

There was Sitting Bull squatting alone in the corner with his calumet, with his large square face—burned brown as an old boot—furrowed by ancient, deeply etched lines, decked out in his best feathers, softest, whitest buckskins and flat-brimmed plainsman's hat.

Buntline with his ruddy peasant's face, his quick smile and his eye for the ladies, but for the moment limping painfully on a bad ankle.

The count with his English tweed suit, blackthorn walking stick, briar pipe and gold monocle; and the countess with her Parisian gown, fake jewels and lavish mane of red-gold hair.

Both of them were phony as hexagonal donuts.

In the corner opposite Bull's sat the most feared Indian in two countries, *Goklayeh*—the notorious Apache warrior known to the white-eyes as Geronimo.

He was dressed in immaculte doeskin vest and leggings, both fringed at the seams with human scalps, and in elaborately beaded thigh-high moccasins. This bronco buck with his thick, muscular build and fierce, flashing eyes looked every inch of his infamous reputation—that of a rawboned Apache, the last ferocious holdout of the great Indian nations.

At present, he was scrutinizing a crystal snifter of cognac with puzzlement and consternation. The first two snifters had shattered in his carelessly violent grip.

Clem's eyes moved on to Cody. He was still in his shabby fringed elkskin jacket and battered black sombrero. With his sandy shoulder-length hair and goatee, and the big Walker Colt on his hip, he still looked the part he'd immortalized onstage and in the press: the fearless frontier Indian-fighter.

If one looked more closely, the face bloomed with grog blossoms, and his eyes were a crimson network of garishly broken blood vessels.

Lawyer Hargrove, who was still in his dark silk three-piece, and Father Tibbs, the cowled, black-robed priest, were the enigmas. They were the men who had brought them all here, under the most strained circumstances. From what she had gathered, half the men and woman had fled to the old *monasterio* on the run from the law.

A fact which seemed to delight the escorts no end.

Her eyes carelessly roamed the refectory. This was the monks' social room, their place of dining and entertainment. And indeed, the long polished oak table was lavishly laid out with bottles of vintage Bordeaux—Chateau LaFite, 1855, generally regarded to be *premier grand cru classe* of all time; ice buckets of chilled Monopole champagne and *blanc de blanc;* wheels of Camembert cheese; the excellent sierra sausage of the country, *choriza;* hammered silver pots overflowing with the rich black beluga caviar; thick hunks of *paté de foie gras;* and vast platters piled high with chilis, tortillas and the *pan de campagne.*

Around the table were a dozen high-back armchairs with leather-paddded seats. The walls were lined with ancient books, some of which appeared to be the journals of long-dead monks. The arched door frames, the massive furniture and the dusty illuminated tapestries gave the refectory a monkish but pleasant air.

As Calamity sipped her goblet of champagne and considered another dram of the excellent 1811 "Year of the Comet" cognac, she started to feel at home. She thought, maybe a couple of days here drinking to Sutherland's demise and waiting for the reading of the will wouldn't be so bad after all.

Then it happened. A thick arched door swung open, and in he walked—bigger than Beelzebub and with a grin like polished steel. He wore a *generalissimo's* dress uniform, weighted down with a wagonload of medals, most of which were French.

Hell's own scourge.

Mejico's own cattle prod.

El Presidente, Porfirio Diaz.

53

All heads turned to the legendary Mexican strongman. Hawk-faced, hook-nosed, dark-complected, heavy of head and frame, Diaz in his khaki beribboned drill looked every inch the malignant despot he was said to be. But the grin—which somehow never reached the dead, expressionless eyes—continued to dazzle.

He inventoried the house with a quick all-embracing glance. "Our host certainly raked up the muck," he said amiably.

All they could do was stare, gape-jawed, till Cody found his tongue.

"You got a lot of hard bark on you, walkin' in here like this. I, for one, am not a man of peace."

The smile continued to spell-bind.

"Yet you will restrain yourself, Colonel Cody. As you know, there is much money to be made here, *mucho dinero*. If we are gentlemen. And money—or the prospect thereof—I like to think, makes all men brothers. Money, after all, speaks the universal tongue."

Diaz boldly strode over to the long oak dining table. A bottle of muscadet was chilling in an ice bucket. He poured some into a crystal goblet. He swirled the glass, remarked the fragrance.

"A tantalizing bouquet," he announced to the room.

He took a careful sip.

"Ah, a delicate, self-deprecating *blanc de blanc*. The perfect thing after an arduous journey, is it not so?"

Without waiting for an answer, Diaz spun about, quickly studying the room. Through an open arched doorway, the vast vault of the sanctuary was visible. He jerked to an abrupt halt and stared at it contemplatively, chin resting on palm.

"This place has a wonderful melancholy to it, a feeling of true despair, do you not think? Already I feel closer to His grand design."

"I can put you closer still," Cody said.

Ignoring him, Diaz threw up his arms, spun around a second time and shouted, "Amigos, I feel a lot of love in this room!"

Cody walked up to him and stuck a clenched knuckle-popped fist under his nose. "All you're gonna feel is *this*."

But Diaz snatched the fist out of the air with a surprising ease. Then to Cody's embarrassed dismay, putting down his wine glass, he opened the fingers one by one and studied the hand carefully.

Three nails were missing, and all the fingertips badly scarred.

"Ni-i-i-i-ce," Diaz said, stretching the word out to five syllables. "But I must say, you do need a new manicurist. Who does your nails anyway?"

"Your late *majordomo* used to do them. In front of you and Sutherland, as you recall. Before Torn Slater shot him."

Diaz abruptly dropped Cody's hand, and for a split second Cody saw the smile waver.

"Thought of Slater shakes you a little, huh?" Cody said.

Diaz shrugged. "I don't see why. From what I hear, he's changed considerably. Instead of the big bad gringo gunman, I hear he's just a pimp. Or maybe 'wimp' is a better word. I hear he has his nose planted squarely in the ass of one of our local border-town *putas* and even the delectable Miss Calamity can't get it out."

He glanced over at Clem as if seeking confirmation.

She nodded unhappily. "Claims he's tryin' to reform her."

"What?" Diaz looked ready to explode with laughter.

"That's what I say." Clem frowned. "He's out there right now, chasin' after some ass-shakin' little slut, clearly out of his mind."

Suddenly, Diaz threw his arms up again and announced jubilantly: "Ah, my friends, you'll never know how much I've missed you. I hope you'll all come to look on *Madre Mejico*," Mother Mexico, "as your home away from home and on myself as the kind of older brother...no, father figure that none of you were ever fortunate enough to have."

Cody thrust a scarred right hand under Diaz's nose, then cocked it into a hard fist.

"Speaking of which, I ain't had a proper chance to thank you."

He turned and swung, throwing the punch off the

pivot, every ounce of his 210 pounds behind the walloping roundhouse right.

Diaz caught the fist in midair.

Then calmly returned it to Cody.

Alongside his heart.

"Please, Mr. Cody," Don Porfirio said softly, still clutching the fist, "stop flexing your muscles. Let bygones be bygones. I want you to look on your previous stay in *Mejico* as merely a stern rite of passage which has left you perhaps a little sadder but infinitely wiser. After all, it was not something which turned your hair white overnight; but, let us say, a soft, flattering lemon-blond."

"What you and Sutherland did to me—"

Diaz cut him off. "What I did to you, let me assure you, *that* you are in no position to do anything about. And as for Sutherland? Go to a séance and bark at him like a dog. If you're so inclined. For that is all you can do. Sutherland is history. He's in the archives. He's returned to the proverbial dust. In short, he is dead. You are the present. The new present. And I, to be more precise, am the new *Mejico*."

Cody glanced down. He noticed that Diaz still held his fist. He tried to shake off the powerful grip.

He couldn't.

Diaz's grin was scintillating. "It is said, first comes arrogance, then knowledge, then understanding, then wisdom. In the end, wealth and power. I plan on going straight to the last two."

He politely released Cody's throbbing fist.

Gloomily, Cody began to work and stretch the aching fingers.

54

Dinner was over, and the cuisine had continued to be excellent. Veal sizzling in Madeira, fresh asparagus, two kinds of wine—a red and a white.

The guests now stood around the refectory table, sipping cognac. The conversation, which had finally worked its way around to Sutherland, seemed to energize Diaz.

"I don't care what any of you say. I wish Sutherland were with us right now," Diaz exclaimed.

"He set world-class records for grue, gore, torture and death," said Calamity.

"Precisely so," agreed Diaz. "A giant lived in that body, and we do miss him, don't we? Who can forget that hearty laugh, that quick, wicked wit, that vast volcanic voice which rang the very rafters. True, I myself shall be infinitely richer and far more powerful politically with his passing, but I still can't get over it. You know, I actually feel something resembling...resembling...well, sentimentality."

"Not grief or emotional loss?" Calamity said, trying to help Diaz find the exact words.

"Those are emotions," Diaz said with a disarming grin, "which, I fear, I am more familiar with in the breach than in the observance."

"Is it true that Sutherland was a despicable sadist?" The countess's voice was derisive.

"In a word, yes."

"Sutherland had a dossier of violence," Buntline said, "that would have sickened Sodom and made Caligula look like a cloistered nun."

"Indeed. He was a satanic seer, an oracle of horror. Just thinking about him reminds me what genius the man had."

"A genius for pain," Cody said. "Speaking of which, whatever happened to that McKillian woman? How does she fit into his will?"

Diaz shook his head disdainfully. "She was probably left out. Oh, I would like to say that she was to Sutherland as Petrarch's Laura, Poe's Vee, Dante's Beatrice. But in all candor, mere sex seldom swelled his manhood. Loving one's neighbor he always dismissed as a code for cretins, and I fear he felt the same about sexual love. I doubt she ever jolted his manhood with the thundercrack of orgasm. Her sumptuous breasts, breathtaking legs, waist-length flame-red hair, her husky, voluptuous voice—they were all lost on the poor boy. His was, in truth, a *psychopathia sexualis*."

"How did he get his excitement?" the count asked.

"Our late friend thrilled to the demented spasms

of a maniac's lust. Murder, torture, theft, castration, dismemberment. These were how he got his kicks."

"You left out money," Buntline remarked.

"Yes," Diaz recalled fondly, "it was often said of him that he would have stolen a red-hot stove. And that was only one of the many things I admired about him."

"The Sutherland I knew practically dotted his *i*'s with dollar signs," Buntline said glumly.

"But of course. The hoarding of wealth was, for Sutherland, one long, riotous, unending fuck, all discharge and orgasm; but, I am afraid, no catharsis or relief."

"In the end he found God," Calamity sneered.

"I wish you hadn't reminded me." Diaz brooded. "Of course, I blame it all on this new-fangled Romanticism sweeping the hemisphere."

"Romanticism?" Cody was incredulous.

"Yes, that deranged doctrine which falsely holds that love can overcome greed, power, war and death. That sentimentality is stronger than hatred, jealousy and revenge."

"What's wrong with that?" Father Tibbs asked.

"Sir, that is the dogma of a lunatic asylum. And believe me, these Romantics in *Mejico* get just what they deserve. Our penal mines and labor colonies cure them of all such misconceptions quickly and thoroughly."

"You cannot kill an idea," Father Tibbs argued, irate. "You can't stop men from thinking."

"Perhaps." Diaz shrugged. "But I can shatter the jawbones on both sides of their skulls and stop them from talking. I can break their fingers and arms and stop them from writing. I can castrate them like steers and stop them from passing their seed to future generations. I can stop them from spreading this demented drivel."

"You, sir, are a black-souled sadist," Buntline exploded.

"And you, sir, are a fourth-rate, no-talent hack," Diaz scolded, shaking a finger at Buntline. "I've read your books, you know."

"You didn't like them?" said Buntline, genuinely hurt.

"They really are quite dreadful. Are you sure you can't find something else to do? God's thunder, man, you *should* give it up."

Calamity fixed Diaz with a tight stare. "Just out of curiosity, what are *you* doing here?"

"I was on a pilgrimage to Mecca and stopped off for a little fun," Diaz said lightly.

"And?" Clem asked, stone-faced.

"And I came down here for the company. Yes, for the discourse. It is most stimulating."

"You came to see *us*?" the countess said with disbelief.

"I came for the fucking money, you stupid clucks," Diaz roared. "I *am* getting the lion's share, you know."

"But Sutherland promised most of his fortune to the Holy Mother Church," said Father Tibbs.

"In *Mejico, I* am the Holy Mother Church."

The group stared at him, horrified.

"Sir, you and Sutherland were—and are—monsters," Calamity snorted.

"Indeed. Though in Sutherland's case he never mastered the craft. His opportunities were limited. He was, globally speaking, a tiger in a litter box, a shark in a goldfish bowl. *Mejico* and the U.S. were too new, too undeveloped for him. Now, if he'd had a Russia or a China to run roughshod over—countries with real *hat-size*—just imagine what bloody horrors he might have wrought. As it was, his gruesome bliss never peaked. His tiger's lust languished."

"What did Sutherland want from you and *Mejico*?" Calamity asked.

"He only wanted to grind the faces of my poor. Considering how much money we made, I was satisfied. Anyway, how could I object? You may be surprised to learn this, but my personal nature is a violent one. And I could work with the man. We understood each other. We thought the same way. These demented democratic do-gooders in your own country, what with their mindless moralizings about freedom, justice and labor reform—they would have disestablished my very economy. Agriculture, industry, all."

"All of which are run on slave labor," Cody reminded him.

"And rightly so," Diaz said with a bright smile. "My *peones* deserve no less."

"In America, we believe in the free flourishing of the individual," Buntline disagreed.

"But what does that do for me? How does that help old *numero uno*, number one?" Diaz asked.

"In the end, Sutherland recanted that obscene philosophy," Father Tibbs said.

"Yes, and how it sickened me. To see that once-great man dressed in sackcloth and ashes, to hear him in a shrill, shrieking voice preaching apocalypse and damnation, well, it was a severe disappointment. As it is, I choose to remember him as he once was—a golden boy of summer, a true sun god—though now he is gone."

Diaz daintily rubbed a tear from his eye.

"Informed critics say that *Mejico*'s national bird is lice," Cody cracked. "They say your *federales* are nothing more than hired thugs."

"And I say that these informed critics are mental defectives and sexual degenerates."

"Please, Don Porfirio," Cody said impatiently, "we've dealt with your *federales*. They are thugs."

Diaz's grin glittered with disdain. "In the interests of public relations, we call them 'Heroes of the Revolution.'"

"How can you tolerate such injustice?" Buntline asked.

"My dear, *Mejico* is a Catholic country. We believe in redemption through pain. Without it, there is no confession and expiation; without pain, we are damned. Perpetually. I, for one, believe my people can still be saved. I shall save them, too. But most painfully, I am afraid."

"That is gutter philosophy," Cody said. "Your people shall surely rebel."

"No, doubt," said Diaz, nodding his head, suddenly saddened at the prospect. "But even now when it is shockingly difficult to get good help, I can persuade my *peones* to perform such truly difficult tasks. The list would stupefy your so-called labor-management experts."

"Don Porfirio," Calamity said, "your own mother must curse the day she gave you birth."

"Yes, but luckily I do not share your exalted love of motherhood. And for the moment, like the late *Señor* Sutherland, I only wish to grind the faces of my poor. For money. It is not too much to ask."

55

As they threaded their way through the twisting maze of canyons toward the searing void of the Great Sonoran Sink, Stanley studied his friends. To say that they suffered from the broiling heat was a grotesque understatement. The Sonoran canyonlands were the hottest spot on God's—or rather, the devil's—bleak earth. Hotter and drier than the Kalahari, than the Sahara, than Death Valley itself in the dead-hot hell of summer. The canyonlands were a nightmare-inferno, Satan's own frying pan.

Stanley glanced down at his shirt and pants. He felt the air steaming inside his Stetson's crown. He was not only unsure how much more he could take, he was doubtful as to how much more his clothes—or his friends' equally distressed clothing—could stand. His collarless brown shirt, frayed Levi's and tan, battered Stetson were heavy with sweat and alkali dust. His square-toed calfskin boots were rundown at the heels. His red bandanna had long since rotted away. His last pair of socks had disintegrated on the trail the fourth day out.

And the trip had been hard on the stock as well. Lathered along the saddle's edges, snorting and blowing foam, even with the best care in the world, they were cracking under the strain. Half the time they had spent walking their mounts, in a feeble attempt to save them, but Slater doubted it had done much good.

Toward the end, the canyon grew narrower, and the last mile was little more than a crevice. Still, they pushed on. Hand-leading their mounts and hazing the pack mules through the tight crack, they found their egress and left the canyonlands in their doomed and luckless wake.

And they entered the Great Sonoran Sink.

56

Henry Morton Stanley was no newcomer to danger, death or to the wilds of nature. He had fought for the Congo Free State, discovered the source of the Congo River deep in equatorial Africa and had tracked down Livingstone in an uncharted land rife with headhunters and cannibals. He had traveled all over the wild West, through hostile Indian country and the toughest hurrah towns the continent had to offer.

Still, he had never witnessed anything like the Great Sink. As they made their way out of the canyon, it was as if they had stepped out onto the moon. This was a sprawling sagebrush void, an empty monotony—unrelieved save for the distant buttes of black lava, the random scattering of obsidian chimneys, the endless unattainable cliffs shimmering in the blurred heat-haze along the desert's rim. Here and there an occasional mesa rose up with thick striated layers horizontally striping the walls. These "breaks" were once the high-water marks of ancient lakes and rivers; and before that, part of a long-forgotten ocean floor.

Now the sink was empty as the Pit, meaningless as the Martian moons. Except for one looming landmark. A half-day's ride, there it was: vibrating in and out of focus in the dead-hot desert air, towering one mile straight up.

Bigger than Beelzebub, prouder than Satan, wickeder than the vilest sins of darkest hell.

The sheer walls of *Sierra de la Noche*.

57

Late that morning they reached the foot of the mountain. Leaving Deacon to tend to the stock, they continued afoot. Scrambling wearily up the loose talus slope, Stanley looked back longingly at the comfortable camp in their wake.

On and on they climbed, up one ghost of a trail after another. Little more than a few treacherous hand- and footholds, each crumbling path seemed narrower than the last; each leaned vertiginously over the precipice side of the mountain. By midafternoon—faces streaked with dust, clothes weighted down with dirt and sweat—they came to it, a narrow cave entrance between a jumble of wagon-size boulders: death's abyss.

With bull's-eye lanterns, candles and pitch torches, they climbed inside.

Corredor de los murcielagos.

The Cavern of Bats.

58

One look inside, and Stanley was ready to turn in his traces and head back. They all were. The dim light in the cave was murky at best, but with the help of their torches and lanterns, they could make out the spectacle overhead, some eight hundred feet up the sinkhole.

They were unnerved by what they saw. *Desmodus rotundus*, suspended from the ceiling. Meaning, bats.

By day they roosted, and by night they hunted ravenously. Three hundred and fifty thousand of them, hanging inverted, crazed with blood hunger.

Such massive bat colonies were not uncommon. Many of the New Mexican caves harbored millions of *chiroptera*, hundreds of species in all. Fox, milk, fruit, javelin, horseshoe, leaf-nosed, slit-faced, hare-lipped, free-tailed, bent-winged, long-legged and the mouse-eared bats. This horde, however, was *Desmodus*.

Pure vampire.

From the colony rained a steady deluge of urine and excrement, black as night, sticky as tar. It collected in a vast pitchy pool 950 feet below the roost. The ammoniac stench from that gaping sink was devastating.

Stanley peered over the brink. Again he wished he hadn't. The pit below was a devil's cauldron bubbling with life, a horrifying blood stew of piss, feces, insects, reptiles—animal life of every repulsive shape and description. For as noxious as the guano may have been to humans, to those scavengers who fed on it and to those predators who hunted them, it was a deluge of nutrition—twenty-five percent pure protein.

So the creatures in the guano pit grew to astonishing proportions: Eight-foot diamondbacks; two-foot centipedes; foot-long spiders, scorpions and beetles. The slime teamed with moiling killers.

Erupting out of the virulent drink were massive stalagmites a hundred feet high, broad as freight wagons. They were inky-hued from the endless shit-rain, and crawling with predatory beasts.

If there was ever a hell, Stanley knew this was it.

He assumed they would head back, when to his horror and dismay, Torn Slater unlimbered a hundred feet of wire-cored climbing line and snaked a long swirling loop across the sinkhole. On the third toss he roped a rocky outcrop. He belayed his end around a heavy granite spire and turned to face the crew.

"The line's guaranteed for a thousand pounds. We each have belt clips to hook us on. I'll cross first and climb back for anyone else with a second line if I have to." He clipped himself to the rope and said,

"Two recommendations: don't look up, and don't open your mouths."

Hanging from the line by his hands and feet, Slater started over the abyss.

Waiting at the precipice's edge, Stanley had never been so terrified in his life. He let everyone go ahead of him—Paxton, Carpenter, Belle, Rozanna, plus all their gear.

On the one hand, this was the generous thing to do. With each passing moment, the rope not only grew slipperier, but the bats overhead—which were roosting, fighting and mating furiously—grew increasingly hostile.

When Stanley's turn came, the vampires were shrilling nervously, puzzled at the disturbance below.

Paralyzed with terror, it was all he could do to clip on the belt lock and swing out over the void into the blinding cyclone of bat shit.

With downturned eyes and clenched teeth, he worked his way through the noxious hurricane. The snakes, centipedes and scorpions in the guano pit were writhing and jumping in the pitchy ooze, and the bats overhead continued to flap, scream, carouse and mate.

Then it happened.

Three-quarters of the way across the abyss, he looked up and saw it. It appeared to him first like a black bloody mortar dropping from the sky—except that this shell had a wingspan of nearly two feet.

The bat barreled into his breadbasket like a flapping, shrieking howitzer. It scratched and crow-hopped across his belly, glaring at him with bloodshot insane eyes, whiskered cheeks, a flat nose and long corrugated ears.

As the blazing orbs fixed him viciously, Stanley also noted that a newborn bat was clinging to the mother's breast with hooked milk teeth and arched claws. The mothlike baby wings were trembling hysterically.

The bat was a mother, Stanley realized in horror.

Then, to his undying fright, a long red tubelike tongue uncoiled from the back of the head; and two sharp, hooked incisors unfolded from the roof of the mouth. The flapping and screaming of the colony overhead accelerated, and then the fangs were all the way out.

A scream tore out of Stanley's throat. He released both rope and bladder and hung helplessly from the clip, back-arched over the abyss.

Suddenly, Slater's Colt flashed, roared and smoked, and Stanley saw the bat detonate in a sickening explosion of fangs, flesh and blood.

His last clear memory was of the bat tumbling talon-over-wings. It landed with a ghastly *whop!* and a splashing horde of shit-swimming vermin swarmed over it. Instantly the bat was gone.

Then he remembered nothing—nothing save the faint recollection of a big dark-haired man with massive shoulders and the flattest, blackest eyes he'd ever seen in his life swinging out over the abyss hand-over-hand.

And hauling him back from the very mouth of hell.

59

When he came to, he was up-shaft. They had broken through the tunnel's barricade, resealed it with scree and deadfall, and were once again safe from the bats.

After they reached a vast, barn-size mining stope, they stripped their ruined clothes, cleaned themselves with the rest of their water and scrubbed each other down, inside and out, with some excellent medicinal brandy.

The ammoniac stench of the guano began to dissipate.

60

After a short rest, Slater started them back up-tunnel. On and on, they picked their way through the abandoned mine shafts. In the eerie light of the guttering candles and the bull's-eye lantern, their faces gleamed dementedly, their eyes huge as saucers. Everywhere they turned in the shafts and drifts, they were surrounded by debris. Broken shoring timbers; fallen ceiling rock; deadfall of every description.

Still, they plunged on. They reached the main stope, that vast cavern which lay less than an hour from the old *monasterio* wall.

Now they needed a rest. Topside, it was still daylight, and they wanted to hit the redoubt after dark. Furthermore, as Carpenter pointed out, the main stope was a landmark of sorts. It was an ancient catacomb. Beneath the floor was an immense enclosed crypt, into which tyrannical Spanish overseers had hurled their rebellious slaves.

To die.

Along the south wall was its only entrance—a small hole with ancient creaking trapdoor. In it were interred the bones of a thousand long-forgotten slaves.

Many still shackled.

Among their bones crawled tarantulas and scorpions.

And the mine rats snarled and shrieked.

PART XII

I've always believed that if a man's stomach was empty enough or his dick hard enough, he would do just about anything.

—J. P. Sutherland

61

The drinking and carousing lasted through the night and into the next day. As a result, it was only late afternoon, during *cafe con leche*, that Clem, Cody and Geronimo noticed the others were missing.

For a long time.

"Damnit," Cody grumbled, "I figured Buntline and the count to be hung over, but nothing like this."

"I assumed the countess was out stealin' the silverware or somethin'."

"And Bull off in a trance," Geronimo grunted.

Lawyer Hargrove and Father Tibbs were just entering for their post-siesta *cafe*.

"I wouldn't get too upset. No one's leaving without their money," Hargrove said. "And the will won't be read till tomorrow."

"They could still have gotten into trouble," argued Calamity.

"Or lost," Father Tibbs said. "This is not your usual Temple of the Lord."

No one could argue with that.

"One other thing," Calamity said. "Where's all them monks what's been under-fuckin'-foot ever since we got here? They're goddamned gone."

She was right.

They got up to search the old *monasterio*.

62

For two hours they trudged through an interminable labyrinth of winding staircases and twisting corridors, searching everything from the upstairs guest rooms and garrets to cellar storage bins.

Then, at the bottom of the last stone stairwell, they came to an arching door of thick polished oak. It opened into a dark room, and Cody swung their bull's-eye lantern inside.

The dungeon was black as Hades, and along the stone walls, grotesque fiends were garishly frescoed. Some infernal artist had long ago adorned the walls with hell-born beasts and bare-fanged devils, unspeakable demons sporting hideous horns and lurid leers. Obscenely grinning gargoyles, carved high above the stone molding, glared down on them, gleaming wickedly in the flickering lantern light, their eyes glittering, their bodies priapic with lust.

Four massive enigmatic objects in the center of the

dungeon were covered with black shrouds, and when one of the veiled objects groaned, their heads jerked toward it. But when they started to approach the groaning thing, a voice from the back of the darkened room thundered: "Stop!"

In the dim lantern light, Cody watched as a dozen black-cowled monks armed with repeating Winchesters closed in on them. Only one priest hung back, a strange, ghoulish-looking cleric who hovered ominously in the rear of the chamber.

In an unnaturally deep and resonant voice, he said, "Some of you might wonder what you are doing here. I like to think that God holds for each of us a plain, strong purpose if we only abjure our fleshly yearnings and see His world with clear eyes. What must we do, you ask, to fulfill His holy work? We must cleanse the blood of lust and lies so that sins and yearnings can never torture us again, so that our souls shall be stainless. In short, the gift we seek is our most sacred treasure. Our soul. We come to you as grim reapers. With death's sickle. Astride a pale horse."

The monk strolled to the low, flat object on the left. He jerked off the black shroud. A woman was lying on a low table with a pallet across her chest and legs. The pallet was piled high with bricks. The woman's face, grotesquely contorted with pain, was barely recognizable as the countess's. She lay writhing in agony under the terrible torture device called *Peine Forte Et Dure.*

The monk strode to the next object and ripped off the shroud. Still upright, but savagely stretched out on a vertical rack by his wrists and ankles, was the count. His eyes were screwed shut against the agony and his teeth clenched in pain.

A fluid sweep of the monk's arm, and the next shroud was flung away. Buntline was strung up by the thumbs from a hanging rack. His mouth was twisted insanely—half grin, half grimace—and his eyes were rolled back till only the whites showed.

The fourth veil was dramatically lifted. Sitting Bull. His wrists and arms were tied behind his back. A rope lashed to his elbows ran through an I-ring screwed into the top of a tall hanging pole. There he hung, hoisted five feet above the floor by his elbows. Strapped to his ankles were rope baskets filled with rocks.

The infamous strappado.

Two wall lamps were lit, and the room was eerily illuminated. Cody could see even more vividly the lurid paintings, macabre carvings and overhead gargoyles—cruel spectators to a season in hell.

The stone floor was covered with sawdust, the apparent purpose of which was to soak up spilled blood. A vast collection of racks, wheels, manacles, two iron maidens and four extra strappados were scattered around the chamber. Three crosses stood in the corners: the four-armed *crux immissa*, the three-armed *crux commissa* and the horrendous *crux decussata*. Under the *crux decussata* was a soaking-wet winding sheet and a filled five-gallon olla—implements of the dread water torture.

The mad monk stepped forward. He raised his arms and threw back the cowl. In a booming, maniacal voice, he shouted:

"As we say in the whorehouse, how's tricks?"

And Cody's jaw gaped.

James Sutherland was back.

63

There was no mistaking the luridly crooked sneer, the flashing eyes, the swath of slick, bone-white scar tissue stretched across the half-bald pate—a notorious *memento mori* from a near-fatal encounter with Outlaw Torn Slater.

Nor could anyone mistake the hail-fellow-well-met laugh or the woman who had just entered, dressed in a nun's habit.

Judith McKillian.

"Now, let's see. We're all present and accounted for, I trust," Sutherland said, swaggering from guest to guest.

With a thrusting index finger he pretended to count the house, pausing here and there to pat a sobbing cheek, ruffle a trembling head. After he'd checked them all, he strode up to Cody, whom he seemed to take special delight in greeting.

"Why, there he is, Bill Cody. Lean, mean and

looking marvelous. Golden ruddy from his ever-glorious day in the sun. Hi there, Billy. Long time no see."

The voice boomed with camaraderie, but the eyes were dead as a three-day carp's.

"Now there's the delectable Calamity. Ummm, looking good enough to eat. And there's that hair-lifting, crow-eating, redskinned sonofabitch, Geronimo. Don't look so tough now, do you, redbelly?" He glanced back at his pain-racked guests, pretending to recount the house with his lone finger. "Countess, Count, Bunty and Bull. Four of a kind and fit as fiddles. But more from you folks anon."

"What is this shit?" Calamity snarled.

"Why, it's the voice of prosperity, ducks. My prosperity, that is. Yours, I'm afraid, is about to take a decided turn for the worse."

"I thought you were dead?" Father Tibbs said, incredulous. "I gave your eulogy. I saw your coffin lowered into Trinity Cemetery."

Sutherland strolled over to the good father, chucked him under the chin.

"Yes, it was quite amusing in that coffin. Eaves-dropping on my allegedly bereaved friends was bloody hysterical. On the downside, the decor was a little grim, especially when as part of the hoax—my con-federates lowered me into that grave. Never thought I'd get out. But then, I gather some of you also got a taste of casket life yourselves. You in particular, Ned," Sutherland said to Buntline, who was hanging just behind him by the thumbs.

Ned's rolled-back eyes fluttered briefly. He hocked and spat, just missing Sutherland's rope sandal.

"Good show, Bunty old boy. I so adore bravery in the face of death."

Sutherland picked a good-size adobe brick from the pile in the room's center. He dropped it into a basket hanging from Buntline's ankles. A sobbing wail tore wolfishly from Buntline's throat, and his eyes rolled back again.

Suddenly, Bull began twitching up and down on the strappado, literally bouncing on the elbow ropes, almost tearing his arms out of the sockets, dramatically escalating the pain. Sutherland walked over to him.

"Spirited buck, isn't he?"

Bull began trilling a slow, singsong up-and-down tremolo. His eyes were shut in ecstasy. He was into his trance.

Sutherland jerked a thumb up at Bull and yelled across the room to another cowled monk. "What's wrong with the Kickapoo? Peyote buttons in the peace pipe again?"

The other monk threw back the hood.

Diaz.

"He's having a mystical experience."

"You mean he *likes* it?" Sutherland was slack-jawed.

Diaz shrugged. "It's part of his religion."

Sutherland stared up at the swinging, lurching, trilling Indian.

"Think it's fun, huh, Mister? Well, listen up. In a few hours we're going to have our own version of the Little Bighorn. The way it *ought* to have been. And let me promise you: This is going to be one long, dark night for your worthless Injun soul. How do you like them apples? I'm going to kick the living buffalo shit out of you."

Bull began bouncing higher, harder. His singsong trills mounted melodiously. He was ecstatically entranced.

"Forget it. We've lost the bloody savage," said Diaz.

"Thinks it's a bleeding sun dance," Sutherland agreed. "Well, he'll heave to before the night's over. He thinks we're sun-dancing, he can think again."

The countess groaned from under the pile of bricks, the hideous *Peine Forte Et Dure* taking its bitter toll.

Sutherland walked up to her and bent over the pile of bricks.

"Say, what's a clean-cut girl like you doing in Sodom and Gomorrah?"

She shut her eyes.

"Oh, I get it. No small talk, huh?"

"What is happening?" she finally groaned.

"We're ruddy well fucked is what's happening," Sutherland said.

"Not *really*?"

"Yes, really. We're going to bounce you around this room like a big ball. Inviolable virtue such as yours should not go unpunished."

"Go fuck yourself, Jimmy," she rasped disdainfully.

"Not only an anatomical impossibility, but also the lesser part of valor."

He dropped another brick onto her pallet, onto the chest from head high.

Ear-piercing howls filled the room.

"Hey, come on, mate," the count called out angrily. "Take it easy on her. That's my wife."

Sutherland strode over to the count, who was decked out in his most exquisite attire. He began fingering the expensively tailored finery.

"I must say, old son, you have a smashing wardrobe. Crisp white silk shirt, French cuffs, dazzling diamonds on the old links here. The complete professional gentleman, huh? What are your net assets, anyway?"

The count looked away.

"Oh, I see. You're wearing them."

He gave the rack's wheel an additional turn.

The count shrieked.

Sutherland strolled over to Buntline, still strung up by the thumbs. Buntline's eyes were rolled back, his mouth working endlessly in a silent, slavering growl.

Sutherland pulled at his pant leg till the growl became gratingly audible. A bleak, blood-streaked pupil appeared, pinning him viciously.

"Don't even bother with him," Diaz recommended. "Buntline has a disgustingly low opinion of everything we've done."

"Why?" Sutherland seemed genuniely puzzled.

He tugged on Buntline's pant leg. Again he groaned.

"He doesn't understand people like us. He wants us all to act like the characters in his novels."

"In his case, stupid, lifeless, two-dimensional characters," Sutherland said.

"In cheap, boring novels," Diaz concurred.

Buntline's eyes lowered and refocused. "Hey, who did you two study criticism under? Torquemada? The Marquis de Sade?"

Sutherland stared at him aghast. He fetched two more bricks and dropped them into the ankle basket.

Buntline passed out.

But now the count was groaning again. "Say, why *are* you going to all this trouble?"

Sutherland shrugged. "What's the point of owning a rack if you don't use it?"

"That's no reason," the countess rasped.

"All right, if you really want to know. But I warn you, the memories may get me sore. The count and the countess? You two ran a phony stock fraud on me and absconded with over forty thousand dollars of *my* money."

He quickly dropped two rocks on the countess's pallet and gave the count's rack two full turns.

For a long moment the room convulsed with their agonizing screams.

Sutherland walked up to Buntline. "Bunty and I were financial partners in Cody's Wild West Show. He got me fired, citing a lack of 'principles.'"

Sutherland dropped brick after brick into the ankle basket, as Buntline wailed hideously.

"So much for principles," Sutherland said lightly.

Sutherland picked out another brick and walked over to Bull, still swinging, bouncing and trilling from the strappado, still entranced.

"Bull and Cody, along with the legendary Outlaw Torn Slater, swindled me out of two priceless pre-Mayan artifacts."

"We got there first," Cody offered by way of explanation.

"It doesn't matter," Sutherland said. "I am not a graceful loser." He stared at Bull a long moment, then tossed the brick back on the pile. "But on the other hand, why waste a good brick?"

"And us?" Clem asked, indicating herself and Geronimo.

"You two gave aid and comfort to my enemy, Torn

Slater; and you helped him plunder my banks, trains and arms shipments."

There was dead silence except for Bull's trills.

"Isn't that reason enough?" Sutherland asked.

Except for Bull, there was still not a sound.

"Well, it was plenty of reason for me," Sutherland said. "Never once over these last years have I forgotten this load of revenge. I realized, to truly satisfy this debt I should have to do you all at once. And how could I get you all here? Simple. Fear and greed. And except for Slater, it worked."

Again, the countess was groaning wretchedly, cracking under her pallet of bricks.

"Please, let us go. Please."

Diaz laughed uproariously.

"What's so funny?" asked Sutherland.

"The thought of somebody expecting mercy from you."

"Precisely so." Sutherland nodded agreeably.

"You unspeakable filth," the count shouted.

"Please don't take it too hard, old stick," Sutherland sneered. "In the grand scheme of things, it shall not matter a whit that you were tortured to death by a sadist."

"This whole episode is most unsportsmanlike," Father Tibbs complained vehemently.

"Thank God!" Sutherland shouted.

"And most uncivilized."

"Really? Would it help matters if I voiced a few pious platitudes *before* torturing these poor buggers? Stuff like *Blessed are the peacemakers? Love thy neighbor as thy self?* That sort of thing?"

Father Tibbs stared at him balefully. "I've made a

terrible mistake." He glanced at Lawyer Hargrove, who merely grinned.

"What's the matter? 'Fraid that Big Guy in the Sky might disapprove?" Lawyer Hargrove snapped.

Sutherland strode over to the pile and fetched an armful of bricks.

"I really fail to see any humor in this," Father Tibbs said.

"Don't worry, Sky Pilot," said Sutherland with a wry smile. "It'll come to you."

64

The torture chamber was a hell of hells, a nightmare's nightmare. The count and countess had passed out cold. Buntline hung by the thumbs with over sixty pounds of bricks strapped to his ankles. Father Tibbs had become so hysterical that Sutherland in a moment of anger had racked him himself.

A few moments on the rack brought the priest under control.

Only Bull seemed immune to the torment. He continued to bounce ecstatically from the strappado, trilling his singsong chants and incantations, oblivious to everything around him.

"Hmmm," mused Sutherland, now staring at the unconscious husband and wife. "Can't have these two missing out on the merriment. No fun in that."

He motioned two monks to get the olla of water. They splashed it in their faces, and the couple came to, groaning.

Sutherland walked over to Buntline, who hung unconscious by his thumbs. He patted Ned's cheek. When there was no response, Sutherland nodded to the monks. They proceeded to splash water in his face, and Buntline's eyes jerked open with a start.

Judith McKillian giggled shrilly.

"Fuck you," Buntline growled at her.

"Gentle now," Sutherland said. "I wouldn't juggle her up. She's not as understanding as myself. You ruddy Yanks are rude, you know, and she'll teach you a nasty lesson in humility."

"There's some things men don't do to one another," the countess groaned.

Her face was terribly white, and she was bleeding from the mouth and ears.

"Really?" Sutherland was skeptical. "I've always believed that if a man's stomach were empty enough or his dick hard enough, he would do just about anything."

"I don't understand any of this," the count rasped.

"That's because it requires the artist's eye." Sutherland observed the count at arm's length over a protruding thumb, as if determining perspective. "Like right now. All I really need is a brush and palette. You now. Live mass. Color. Curve. Hue. Tension. Proportion. Composition. And then I'd have it. A true work of art. Beauty is truth; truth, beauty." He sneered at the spread-eagled count. "We could call the composition *Rack-of-Man*."

Diaz strode over to Sutherland's side.

"You know, my friend," he said, "this is grand fun, but I do wish we had *Señor* Slater here."

"Yes, I would have loved that. However, enough whining. We do have these good people. And take my word, tonight shall not find them banging their tankards in raucous good cheer. This night we shall touch them to the pits of their souls, to the bottomless well of those loathsome wombs in which they were born."

"If only we had Slater."

"There's always tomorrow."

Diaz brightened visibly. "Who knows what *mañana* will bring?"

65

The count had fainted once again. The countess was doing badly indeed. To get her attention, Sutherland slapped her face twice, forehand, backhand.

"'Compulsion?'" Sutherland orated in ringing tones. "'Zounds, were I at the strappado, or stretched on all the racks of the world, I would not tell you upon compulsion.' Tell me, ducks, you believe that? Could we really wrench confession from a sinner with these infernal machines? Well, tonight we shall find out. And please, ducks, let's have some honest emotion. None of your fishing for false sympathy or crocodile tears or pseudo-sobs. None of your usual boring bullshit."

But there was no response. *Nada.* Sutherland bent at the waist. Wrapping the countess's magnificent Titian-hued tresses in his fist, he jerked her hair hard. Once. Twice. Three times.

Nothing.

Diaz strode up to him. "I have some rather bad news for you, my friend. The bitch has passed on." He patted Sutherland on the shoulder in mock consolation.

"Ah, well, she wasn't much in her prime. And she's nothing dead." Without a twinge of doubt or dismay, he spun around and turned to her unconscious husband stretched on the vertical rack, and more water was splashed in the count's face.

Miraculously, the count still held the gold-rimmed monocle firmly in his eye. He squinted through it a hard minute, trying to focus.

"You got a weird haircut, fella," he said, staring at Sutherland's half-scalped pate with a puzzled expression. "Say, this is a great rack. You wouldn't consider selling it, would you?"

He passed out again.

Sutherland slapped his cheeks. Once, twice, three times. The eyes opened, the monocle still miraculously in place.

"You're in death's teeth, bucko. You know, the prospect of dying is supposed to 'wonderfully concentrate the mind'? Do you think so?"

Again, the count fainted.

Again, more water and more groans.

"Say, Count, what do you think hell is like?"

"Rather like a crashingly dull dinner party, I suppose."

"No doubt. In which case you'll have me to thank for not letting your last moments on earth be boring."

The count gave him a knowing wink, then whispered to Sutherland conspiratorially, "We're all grown-ups here. Let me make you a proposition. I have this little niece. Nine going on ten. A fetching little thing, really. Her mother died, and her father—my brother—well, quite frankly he's in prison. She's my blooming property. I *own* her. And she could be all yours. Just for the asking. Every delectable inch of her."

Sutherland gave the stretching wheel two more turns, and again the count passed out, blood trickling from his nose and ears.

It took half an *olla* of water to revive him.

"I sincerely wish you'd stop that, old stick. It really smarts, you know. More than that, it's utterly unnerving. I said, don't—"

Sutherland turned the wheel again.

"Unnnnnhhhhh—Argrrggghhht! I'm ordering you, you bloody fool—Unnnnnnnnnnhhhhhhh—"

Abruptly, the count's head slumped onto his chest.

Again Diaz approached them. Reaching up to the count's throat, he felt for the pulse.

"Sorry, old scout. I'm afraid your *compadre* has gone to that Great Con Game in the Sky."

"Let him try that stock-fraud scam up there," Sutherland said bitterly.

He strode over to the unconscious Buntline and tugged on his pant leg. Buntline came to, groaning.

"Come on, Bunty. Time to get your gruel."

Buntline was rambling incoherently. "Gentlemen, let me assure you, when it comes to murder, horror, torture and gore, I am the true expert here. This nation's high priest of penny-dreadful death, in fact. So please, allow me. You're doing this all wrong. If you'd only—"

Sutherland dropped two more bricks into his ankle basket.

Buntline screamed and passed out.

Sutherland turned to the others. He motioned to his

henchmen, dressed up as monks. "Room for three more, thanks in part to the countess and count. Fetch the slut. Redbelly too. Give Cody the extra rack. God, how I've wanted to get my hands on him."

Diaz came up behind Sutherland and slapped him on the back. "Haven't we all, *amigo?*"

66

Cody and Clem were stretched out on the two vertical racks.

Geronimo hung beside Bull from a matching strappado.

Sutherland gloated with an ear-to-ear grin. "You know, there is a new naïveté under the sun. People no longer believe in the devil. I intend to change all that. I shall introduce them to him. Personally."

"But that could destroy the whole basis of Western civilization," Cody argued.

"You mean the rack? The wheel? *Peine Forte Et Dure*? No, my friend, they're fine. I've kept them in perfect working order. Right here. For you."

"Yes, and rather anxiety-producing," Buntline slurred disjointedly.

"I certainly hope so," Sutherland said, taking out his watch. "Well, time is of the essence." He grinned diabolically. "We'll start with the honey."

After Clem stopped screaming, Sutherland said: "God, that feels good. You know, in all my life I've never known such peace and contentment."

"You do whip out the old welcome mat," Cody gritted angrily.

"Speaking of which, good friend, I've been waiting to get my tingling talons into you for some time."

"You mean I'm not supposed to survive this little slumber party?"

"Amigo, you are now on the outermost rim of injustice. Blindness, castration, water torture, the wheel, fire and even brimstone shall all rise joyously to greet you. In due course."

Sutherland paused to stroke and pet Calamity's stretching-wheel.

"We could try saying we're sorry," Clem suggested.

Sutherland's sneer was stunning. "Don't worry about it, my dear," he said, chucking her under the chin pleasantly. "Worry leads to hypertension and abdominal lesions. Anyway, we'll all be together in paradise. Soon. Isn't that right, *Padre*?"

Father Tibbs looked away, while Lawyer Hargrove laughed uproariously.

"Here. Allow me to wipe all such anxieties from your mind." He gripped the stretching wheel and grinned at Diaz. "Now let's put some *real* heat under this popcorn popper."

67

It was during her third turn of the stretching wheel that the dynamite charge blew the big arched door to pieces. Calamity would never forget the way it looked. In one split second, the door was vomiting in on them, a deafening explosion of flames, flying debris and black choking smoke.

But with tear-dimmed eyes, she still saw his entrance: Torn Slater, his Winchester—which her ringing, throbbing eardrums could not hear—levering and flashing in his hands, as he charged through the smoke and flames. Carpenter, Paxton, Stanley, Rozanna and Belle Fucking Starr were taking up the rear, and Sutherland's black-cowled rifle-toting henchmen were dropping so fast she couldn't believe her eyes.

Diaz, Sutherland and Lawyer Hargrove instantly threw up their hands, while Father Tibbs fell to his knees and, crossing himself rapidly, recited a stuttering host of nonstop Hail-Marys. While Carpenter and

Stanley held them at gunpoint, Slater took out his knife and began cutting her rack ropes.

"Sorry I was late for the will-readin'. Hope I didn't disappoint you none."

"You've never disappointed me," Calamity gasped. "'Cept that time you got sent to Yuma. Or maybe that other time Diaz locked you up in Sonora Prison. Maybe when you took the fall back in Brownsville, and except for leavin' me for that Mex bitch, I—"

Slater caught her as she dropped unconscious from the rack, somehow, someway smiling.

68

They were preparing their departure from that vile *sanctum sanctorum*. The group was in bad shape. Bull limped grotesquely. Buntline couldn't walk at all. Cody was half dead. Clem had been all but broken on the rack.

Still, the sight they left behind them was enough to lighten the sickest man's heart.

Lawyer Hargrove groaning under a staggeringly high pile of bricks on the *Peine Forte Et Dure*.

Diaz, dangling by his elbows from the strappado, his sobbing howls echoing through the night.

The shrieking McKillian woman strung up by the thumbs.

Sutherland spread-eagled on the rack, screaming like a banshee in hell.

Geronimo sat at the stretching wheel, tightening Sutherland's ropes.

Pausing only to drop extra bricks into Diaz's ankle baskets.

And to grin dementedly.

"Are you sure it's safe to leave him behind?" Clem asked.

"Don't worry. Them Comancheros are in the bottom of the gorge. You can see them from the bell tower. They're drunk, hung over and still bedded down. It would take them a good six hours to hike up here anyway, so he can keep an eye on them. Geronimo's got ten hours' working time, minimum."

"Can he find his way back?" Clem asked, still not convinced.

"He lives down here. He can find a hundred ways down this mountain. He's probably better off without us."

Only Bull seemed distraught.

As they left, Clem noticed him staring at the strappado.

It was as if he'd left part of himself on that wretched machine.

As she shut the door behind them, she took one last look at that house of horrors.

Geronimo was giving the rack's stretching wheel two hard turns.

To Sutherland's undying screams.

69

What had originally taken them a few hours now dragged on and on and on. Half the crew was barely ambulatory. Buntline and Clem had to be carried most of the way. Part of the tunnel had collapsed after the last trip, and they had to dig their way through it.

Still, twelve hours later, one hour before nightfall, they reached the bat cave. The rope was still strong, and Deacon was waving them across.

"We best haul ass. Them Comancheros don't catch up with us, the bats will for sure. Paxton, Carpenter, Belle—you two get over there. I'll ferry the rest across. We got to move."

70

Deepening dusk filled the sinkhole. All Slater's people had crossed the pit and were heading down the trail. Except for Buntline. His thumbs were swollen to three times their normal size, and he was now delirious, slipping in and out of consciousness. He was utterly unable to even reach the rope, let alone crawl across.

As twilight shadowed the pit, the bats shrieked and stirred. Slater swung back over the abyss, hand over hand. He hoisted Buntline up by the legs, lashed his ankles over the rope, then his wrists. After latching his belt clip to the rope, Slater himself swung back across the pit, hauling Buntline after him.

In the gathering gloom the bats were beginning to swoop and trumpet furiously. The colony felt the call of night and the frantic gnawing of blood-hunger. Eager to be off, the more adventurous vampires dived at the slick guano-blackened rope along which Slater dragged the unconscious Buntline. Occasionally the creatures lashed out with fang or claw; and while, for the most part, Slater was able to kick or slap them away, Buntline endured the bloody slashes, limp and comatose.

Deacon was still on the other side, and helped Slater unhook the unconscious Buntline. The colony overhead was growing increasingly violent, and the cave was darkening rapidly. Deacon seemed especially eager to get down the mountain. Then, glancing over his shoulder, Slater saw him.

Swinging hand over hand across the rope, bats swooping on him with desperate fury, came Geronimo. Even before he was halfway across, he shouted to Slater:

"The black-robe called Tibbs. You said not to harm him? He repaid your kindness well. He sneaked down the mountain to those *hideputas* Comancheros. Luckily, I went to the bell tower later and spotted them on the slope. I came straight to the shaft to warn you."

"You mean they're on our trail?"

"Enju." Yes.

By now Geromino was across, and Deacon was pulling him up onto the ledge. "You boys just get movin'," he said, slinging Buntline up over his shoulder. "I got a surprise for them what's on your back-trail, something I cooked up special. Providin' we can haul ass off this mountain 'fore them bats get out of here."

71

They reached Clem and the rest just as the first long rope of bats came roiling out of the mountain like a coil of black smoke. They were slightly more than a quarter mile from the slope, but even so the blast hit them with a stomach-churning jolt. The dynamite's *ka-whumppp! ka-whumppp! ka-whumppp!* echoed and slapped off mountainside, booming across the Great Sonoran Sink like rolling thunder. The shock waves rumbled through the void, scattering grit and gravel in all directions. Their stock and mounts were bucking and rearing, and the jerk-line mule string—too snuffy and spooked to be led—was braying, kicking savagely. In fact, the lead animal bolted, to which Deacon shouted: "Let him go."

By now Calamity's rearing roan was bucking out of control, but even as she fought the reins and clung to the apple, she could not help but stare jerkily at the distant mountain slope, frightened yet mesmerized. The upper half of the cliff-face hung suspended, hovering there halfway up the mountain for a seeming eternity, then slowly cracking loose in a colossal burst of flame, crashing into the Great Sink with a *boom*! just as Clem piled off the roan.

A case of dynamite, planted in a thin black obsidian fault line halfway up the mountainside, had brought down most of the slope, sealing off the *corridor de los murcielagos*, the infamous cavern of bats.

Forever.

72

Flynn didn't like his job. He didn't like it one bit. Leading this filthy, drunken Comanchero band through an endless maze of collapsing dust-choked tunnels after Slater's gang was not the sort of deal he'd bargained for. Two of his men had already died in a cave-in; the rest were on the verge of mutiny; and he himself, quite frankly, had had it. Then after that last colossal ear-cracking mine-quake, he called his troops to a halt. He went back to the main stop to talk it over with his boss.

There he heard the up-tunnel commotion. He did not know which surprised him most, his men screaming and sobbing, cursing and wailing, or what came next: the sight of that first bat—that first flat-nosed, slant-eyed, bare-fanged vampire flashing past his face and swooping down on Hargrove's neck while the lawyer thrashed and screeched hysterically.

If, however, Flynn found either of those events a

shock, it was nothing compared to what he witnessed next. It began as a distant, muted scream. Slowly it overwhelmed the sobbing howls of his men, then silenced them with an abrupt breathless hush. It was followed by an intense roar rather like that of a cyclonic wind, followed by a random attack of more shrieking fiends, followed by what Flynn could only describe as a vast sudden wall of murderous bats— flat-faced, almond-eyed, fanged, shrilling like all the banshees in hell.

Flynn was speechless, paralyzed with terror, and would have died on the spot except that the McKillian woman found her voice.

One word.

"Catacombs!"

By now the bat colony was all around them, slashing, tearing, rending, mad with blood-hunger. They were getting ripped to pieces by the hideous beasts. When, without even thinking, Flynn was tumbling head over heels after the rest as they literally dived into the *oubliette*'s opening, pulling the trapdoor shut.

Trapping them and dozens of blood-crazed vampires which had followed them in there.

Trapping them with the shackled bones of a thousand long-dead slaves.

Trapping them and the ravenous horde of marauding mine rats.

And there Flynn waited, fighting off the swooping bats and shrieking rodents.

And overhead, an army of trumpeting vampires battered the rickety trapdoor.

PART XIII

I love you, *gringo*, no shit.

—Rozanna Morales

73

In the Nogales cantina they waited for the next train. Since it came only once a week—if it came then—Slater had plenty of time to brood.

Not that he was all that uncomfortable. There was plenty of mescal. Lots of *cerveza frio*—ice-cold beer—chilled in the cantina well. Good companionship. Lots of *frioles* and *tostados* and *mole poblano*.

No, the thing that got on Slater's nerves was the Professor. Paxton had located a concertina, and all week he'd regaled them with his songs, most of which were about Slater. Such as the one he was singing now. "Yuma Jail" from the "The Ballad of Outlaw Torn Slater." In a raucous spirited voice, he sang:

You're Outlaw Torn Slater, train-robbin's your game,
Though you hit some banks with Frank and Jesse

DEVIL'S STING

James.
Cole Younger like to share in your fame.
But there's hell to pay on your back-trail.
Them wanted posters say "no-hope-of-bail"
In Yuma Jail.

Well, you rode in the war with Bloody Bill
And an outlaw-guerrilla named Colonel Quantrill.
Now all them boys gone to Texas or hell.
Say, why's them lawmen climbin' your tail?
And them bitches you abandoned, Lord, listen to
  them wail
In Yuma Jail.

Now you jumped the fence and you're on the run
After sendin' a guard to Kingdom Come
For callin' you "that hillbilly scum"
Now a floggin' post's awaitin' your tail
And a hard-rock pile's on your back-trail
In Yuma Jail.

Long wailin' whistle through your soul it's throbbed
For the men that you killed and the trains that you
  robbed.
For the banks that you hit and the women that
  sobbed.
It's followin' you, boy, up your back-trail.
Don't look back, boy, just listen to it wail
Back in Yuma Jail.

Slater was not amused by Paxton's virtuosity, nor
did he appreciate the notoriety which the professor's
nationwide hits were bringing him. As Slater was
quick to point out, fame in his line of work was little
more than suicide.

Not that anyone else shared Slater's delicate sensitivities. The rest of the crowd loved the raucous, hard-driving music. They pounded on the cantina tables, yelled, whistled and shouted:

"Bravo!"

"Ole!"

"More! More!"

Periodically, Slater took his friend aside and attempted to reason with him. He complained bitterly that he didn't want Paxton "writin' no more songs 'bout him." He was "sick of hearin' that shit every time he walked into some no-'count hell-town brothel-saloon." Slater would restate his equation between fame and suicide, to which Paxton would nod his head seriously and, solemn as a boiled owl, agree. But somehow, someway, before the day was out, someone somewhere would ask him to play. He would forget, and soon would be singing the fateful songs again.

Even worse, his woman Rozanna was constantly on his back. In fact, right now she was again summoning him to the upstairs bedroom. In a shrill voice, she shouted from the second floor landing:

"Torn? What is wrong, *amigo*? Why you no up here with your *chiquita*?"

Slowly, haltingly, Slater limped toward the steps.

74

Slater wasn't the only one who was out of sorts.
While the others drank, danced and sang, Sitting
Bull sat in a corner, smoked his calumet and brooded.
The music, of course, had no more meaning to him
than the Martian moons, and he always abstained
from spirits. But those weren't the reasons he ig-
nored the festivities.

It happened that night in the old *monasterio*. While
the strappado had not been as effective as the sun
dance, still it had hurt sufficiently to provoke a
vision. But what kind of vision? *That* was the question.
Bull had seen his people dressed in white man's
clothing, walking the white man's streets, mingling
with white men, working, laughing, crying, playing.

He had seen the Sioux—meaning, *the* People—
mingling with their obvious inferiors.

As equals.

The thought made Sitting Bull shudder. The vision which he had longed for in his holiest of hearts was a sacred victory in battle, another Little Bighorn, a triumph so decisive that the Sioux would regain their lands and the white spoilers would be driven from the high plains country forever.

Failing that, he had wished for his nation a glorious death in battle. Then they could rejoin their ancestors and, blessed by Wakan Tanka, continue to live, hunt and make sacred war in the Sioux hereafter, the Shadowland.

Instead he saw a world in which his people were reduced to the abysmal level of the earth-scratching, mountain-digging palefaces.

He witnessed a hideous world in which his people— *the* People—no longer hunted the elk and pronghorn and buffalo, but toiled in factories and scarred the sacred earth with shovel and plow, a world in which his Sioux brothers wore shoes, attended schools and even crowded into the white-eyes' church to worship the Christian God.

Wakan Tanka had truly abandoned his people. Now Bull could never—like the great white-eyes warrior *O-dys-seus*—plant his oar and find peace.

Bull turned face to the cantina wall, softly chanted his last-song and prayed for his death.

75

But, in truth, Bull's and Slater's problems were petty alongside Buntline's. Among other things, he hadn't written a word in over three months; and the accumulated debts from eight marriages, untold paternity suits, his massive alimony and child-support bills—combined with the exorbitant expense of his obscenely profligate life-style—threatened to bury him forever. The truth be known, Sutherland had racked his thumbs so sadistically, Buntline doubted that his swollen, misshapen digits could ever hold a pen again.

But worse than the physical pain and the prospect of imminent bankruptcy were the fierce wounds to his artistic pride. During the past few months, Buntline had endured a veritable shitload of criticism over his books, and he was sick of it. Buntline was a man with 557 paperback novels under his belt. Why were all these morons suddenly coming out of the woodwork and telling him that his writing stank?

With an aching thumb, he poured himself another drink.

Equally painful was the lack of women. The Nogales whores were so mortally homely that they'd come near to scaring a buzzard off a shit wagon, cause a blood-crazed buck wolf to drop a pork chop, make a freight train take a dirt road.

Again, Buntline grumbled silently to himself and knocked back another shot. He absently glanced around the room, checking out the ladies for the fortieth time that morning. Their own women were otherwise occupied. Belle? She seemed hell-bent on screwing Henry Stanley to death; and Clem, if she couldn't have Slater, had sworn she wouldn't take anyone. Rozanna—that toothsome piece, for whom he would have given his right arm—she seemed determined to break Slater on the inexhaustible rack of her own insatiable lust.

Even now, he could hear the upstairs din of creaking slats, bouncing bed legs and her shrill screams, culminating in a rasping, protracted "EEEE-AAAA-AAGGGGHHHHH!"

But while Buntline sat there and grumbled, half sick with his swollen, throbbing thumbs and his voraciously carnal cravings, even so, he did not envy Slater the wrangles that followed—the endless screams, snarls, slaps, groans and sobs. The two upstairs argued endlessly. Slater railed about a promise he made to her sister—how she "wasn't going to be no whore," and he "sure as hell weren't no pimp." Then he would tell her in no uncertain terms that it was time for him to "get back to his old trade, back to the high lines, the owlhoot trail."

And sure as buzzards eat carrion, they were about to go at it again. Buntline could already anticipate Slater's diatribe by heart: "You aren't going to be a whore! You hear me, girl? You aren't whoring your ass!"

When suddenly, to Buntline's undying dismay, he heard instead: "Go ahead. I don't care what you do. I give up."

Then he heard Slater grumble, roll over and begin to snore.

Suddenly, Rozanna was on the upstairs landing, laughing. To his stunned disbelief, she was combing her hair, grinning, scouting the house, checking out the men.

And staring at *him*.

He tried to look away, but her eyes pinned him. She bounded down the steps three at a time, vaulted the railing and, in one fluid move, was smack in his lap. And to everyone's blank astonishment, she blurted out the first words of English any of them had heard her speak:

"I love you, *gringo*, no shit."

Her hand was in his pants. Was it true love or the pesos in his pockets? Out came a double eagle. She eyed the coin with a cool appraising gaze, chomped down on it knowingly, testing for the gold.

Leaving three wicked-looking fissures in its smooth shiny surface.

With a dazzlingly expansive grin, she took him by the hand and let him up the steps. When he resisted, she grabbed a misshapen, pain-racked thumb and wrenched it hard.

He stumbled and sobbed, limped and whimpered. By the time they reached the landing, his knees were trembling violently. With a no-nonsense twist of the thumb, Rozanna led him, groaning and gasping, into an empty upstairs crib.

Suddenly Buntline recalled, with ghastly clarity, that long-ago night when he'd met Lawyer Hargrove and the priest.

And, once again, he was sorry—heartily, horribly, hopelessly sorry—that he'd ever messed around with Frank Hardy's wife.